enjoy a fiesty Heorine! (in both stories)

♥

Max Billetes
aka Pumpkin Spice

H

Evernight Publishing

www.evernightpublishing.com

Copyright© 2016

Evernight Publishing

Editor: Karyn White

Cover Artist: Jay Aheer

ISBN: 978-1-77233-788-4

ALL RIGHTS RESERVED

PUMPKIN SPICE

DEDICATION

This was always written for a young woman I greatly admire and imagine as a modern-day heroine. She's my Scarlett, with a devotion to family and a passion that is yet to be ignited. Like every young woman she's just waiting for the right hero to come crashing into her life. I know he will, and I can't wait to watch her love story unfold.

To CM, with all my love, Pumpkin

PUMPKIN SPICE

SCARLETT HOOD & THE HUNTER

The Amāre Tales, 1

Pumpkin Spice

Copyright © 2015

Chapter One

Why does she have to live so far from town? The Dark Forest was especially dim this evening. I pivoted on the heel of my boot. The Enchanted Forest tavern faintly glowed behind me.

The Enchanted Forest tavern wasn't actually in the forest, but rather on the outskirts of the merry little town of Amāre. While the tavern was housed in a charming cottage with amber colored-roof shingles and slanted eaves where lanterns hung to light the way for travelers, just beyond its reach lay the Dark Forest. And there wasn't anything enchanted about the Dark Forest. It was a place where even the most skilled huntsman wouldn't travel.

Seriously. Why does she live out here? I stepped around the fallen foliage that scattered the dirt path like strewn matchsticks. I knew the way to my grandmother's house, but there was something in the air that sent a chill throughout my body and settled on my scalp. It felt like someone was watching me. But when I turned in either direction, all I saw were giant sequoias and fir trees that stretched high into the evening sky and surrounded me in green. I shuddered, pulled up my hoodie, and tucked my long, red, wavy hair inside my cap. It did nothing to warm me or change the fact that it was way too late to be traveling to Granny's house alone, but the pink bakery box that was tucked in my backpack and kept pressing into my shoulder reminded me why I was headed there. The bottle of merlot that seemed to swish with every step was the only incentive to keep tracking forward.

"Cake and wine," I said to the black crow that seemed to hop along with me from one tall tree branch to the next keeping me company. "It's the makings for a perfect pick-me-up." The crow took flight and landed on the succeeding limb. Pine needles fell like confetti from the sky and scattered beneath my feet. "Are you following me?" I paused, and for a moment I considered grabbing my camera. But I knew once I pulled it out, I'd lose track of time. It's what always happened when I was off duty from the radio station and shooting for fun.

When I no longer had to photograph for the purpose of the station's online photo gallery that updated listeners to stories we were covering on the air, I could let my mind wander. Something about a deadline seemed to put a chokehold on my creativity, but when it wasn't looming over my head, I was free to let my lens capture whatever it saw. That was the beauty of photography. Through the lens an entirely new world opened up to me. My camera allowed me to see things I normally wouldn't. And I could only imagine what it would spot in the distance as soon as I focused on the raven.

"Can't stop now," I said to the black bird. "Granny's been sick and needs a little cheer me up. And nothing says, 'Get better soon!' than dessert and vino."

"I couldn't agree more."

His voice came out of nowhere. I jumped and screamed in tandem. "What the hell!" The crow flew from its perch, and suddenly I felt very alone with the dark-haired man that stepped out of the shadows of the forest.

"Hello," he said.

"What a deep voice you have!" The startled thought blurted from my mouth.

"The better to greet you with, my dear." He stepped into the light, and I took a step back.

Shit, shit, shit. What do I do? My cell phone was in the front pocket of my backpack, which was slung over my shoulder and out of reach.

His eyes were large and as dark as the raven's. They seemed to bore into me, and I couldn't stop staring.

"Goodness, what big eyes you have!" My thoughts were running random, sporadic, and seemed to fly out of my mouth as soon as I thought them.

"The better to see you with, my dear." The man slowly walked toward me, and I backed away in equal measure. He was sharply dressed in a gray pinstriped suit, crisp white dress shirt, and a silver tie. Definitely overdressed for the forest. *He's not a lumberjack that's for sure. Maybe he's one of the corporate lawyers trying to get the lumberjacks to unionize.*

"I mean you no harm," he said and held up his hands. He palmed an iPhone in his right hand. "If you'd like to call someone." He extended it toward me.

I shook my head. *It's a trap. I don't know what kind of trap, but it's got to be, right? I grab the phone and he grabs me.* "No," I said curtly. "Thank you, but no."

"All right. I understand. I'd be leery, too," he said. "But perhaps you could help me?" His voice softened. "I got turned around in this maze of trees, and I can't seem to find my way back home." He pointed behind him. "I met with a client and then after I left her house." He shook his head, but his perfectly coifed black hair didn't move. "I seemed to have turned right when I probably should've turned left?"

He seemed genuinely confused. Still, I crossed my arms over my chest. There were only a handful of home owners that lived in the Dark Forest. And I knew all of them. They worked with my Granny at the Bunyan lumber yard. "Well maybe I can help," I said. "Whose house were you leaving?"

When he smiled, large, white teeth flashed. "I'm not at liberty to discuss my clients."

I raised an eyebrow. "Well, that's a bummer because if I knew where you were coming from I could help you get back to where you started." *Two can play this game, buddy.* I started to walk away—slow enough that I didn't look like I was scared, but fast enough that he knew I meant business.

"Fair enough," he said to my back.

I kept trudging forward.

"Babe. I was at Babe's house."

I stopped in my tracks. Babe Ox was the love of Paul Bunyan's life. She was the head cook he'd hired to oversee the man camp. And as the legend goes, Babe and Bunyan fell in love during the winter of the blue snow. Theirs was a love affair for the ages. Her wheat cakes and country baked hams were as legendary as his logging skills. When Paul died, Babe inherited the men's bunkhouses, shanty camp, and lumber yard that represented the largest timber supply in North America. Babe's fortune was in the countless millions.

"You were at Babe's house?" The change in my tone couldn't go unnoticed. Babe had become somewhat of a recluse after Bunyan died. The lumber yard practically ran itself, so there wasn't much need for her to participate in the daily operation. According to Granny, Babe only socialized at the monthly Bunco night, and that's only because Granny and her cronies wouldn't let Babe sit home alone night after night. It was highly unlikely that this Mr. Gray Suit was at Babe's house.

"Yes, Miss Ox and I had many items to go over and discuss," he said.

Well I'll give the man street cred for knowing they never married. But still...

"Time got away from me, and when we ended our meeting, the sun was no longer shining to point the way home," he said.

"Uh-huh. Well, if you were coming from Babe's house there was no right or left turn to be taken. Her house is a direct path from the lumber yard. So if you get back on the dirt path and head south," I said and hiked my thumb over my shoulder, "you'll hit the yard and the parking lot within twenty minutes." I rolled my shoulder to distribute the weight in my backpack. It did nothing but cause the bakery box to dig further into my skin. "Have a good night."

I started toward Granny's house. I assumed the mystery man was walking away from me and toward the lumber yard and his car. I assumed wrong.

"Excuse me," he said.

I turned around, and I'm sure my face conveyed my frustration. If it didn't, the agitation in my voice did. "What?"

"I was wondering if you had any extra dessert that you wouldn't mind sharing?" He patted his stomach. "I have not eaten since morning."

"Are you kidding me?" I placed my hands on my hips and took a broad stance against this man. I was, after all, in my favorite calico print skirt that hit just above my knee, and happened to show off my amazing new honey-colored boots that weren't designed for kicking someone's ass, but I'm sure the heel could do the job if I didn't fall first because they were still kind of slick. Didn't matter. I'd gladly scuff my new boots and fall on my ass in the process because this guy was seriously pissing me off. "I don't even know who you are or what you're really doing here."

He took three giant steps in my direction. A long, thin arm extended toward me like a vine unwrapping itself. This man seemed to unfold before me. The top of his hand was covered in thick, dark hair so that I almost mistook it for a glove.

"What big hands you have!" I no longer seemed to care about proper etiquette. Everything I thought flew out of my mouth randomly and at will.

"Ah, the better to help you with, my dear."

His hands were big and hairy. *Ew.* I didn't want to touch him, let alone grasp and shake his hand, but hell if he didn't keep extending his mitt like some peace offering. *Great.*

I quickly shook his hand.

"I'm Bernie Wolfe," he said in his deep, dark voice.

"I'm Scarlett Hood." I quickly withdrew my hand and then tucked it into the front pocket of my hoodie where I tried to wipe away the feeling of all that hair. *Uh. Gross.*

He tilted his head, and dark eyes gleaned under the dawn of moonlight. "As in Wood Hood?" His voice deeper and darker. "The Neighborhood Logging Collective?"

"It's my grandmother's. She founded it."

He slowly nodded. "What a funny, strange coincidence. I was just talking to Miss Ox about your grandmother's cooperative. I thought she sold her shares?"

I loudly exhaled. "Yeah, I don't discuss my grandmother's business with strangers."

His toothy grin filled his face. "Oh, but you see Miss Hood, I'm not just a stranger. I'm friends with Miss Ox."

Yeah, whatever. I hefted my backpack over my shoulder and resumed walking.

"So that dessert?" His voice called out after me.

Fat chance, buddy.

"I thought we could share some of it?"

You thought wrong. I continued to walk away from him.

"Well, that is a shame. I'll have to tell Miss Ox that I was only able to save her from financial ruin and not her dear friend Mrs. Hood."

Rumors had circulated that Blue's holdings were in jeopardy. Tree huggers and environmentalist trying to shut down her mill and lumber yard had wrought havoc on her holdings. But that's all I thought they were— rumors.

"Yes, it will be a shame when your grandmother's hard earned collective is lost," he said. "It will affect many townsmen." His voice drifted toward me like a snake hissing along the ground.

Granny's cooperative had begun when the local lumberjacks complained about their wages. Granny had been cooking beside Blue in the men's camp when the two women drafted the idea of a neighborhood logging collective. The idea was that, like collective farming, the lumberjacks would be compensated not by wages, but by a share of the lumberyard's net productivity. Granny presented the idea to Bunyan, who Blue had already convinced was a better business model for the men in his camp. Bunyan got on board, and the Neighborhood Logging Collective was born. In honor of my Granny

Wood, the lumberjacks nicknamed the Neighborhood Logging Collective, "Wood Hood."

The union had long wanted to disband the logging collective and have set wages. Wood Hood treated the lumberjacks as equals with owners Blue and Bunyan, giving the men a stake in the company. Productivity was tied to their earnings, so it created a win-win for everyone. But the union was persistent. It pushed the men for set wages because if the lumberjacks unionized the union would get a hefty piece of the profit. When Bunyan was alive, he fought off the union wolves. But now that he was dead and Blue was mourning, my Granny was all alone in the war against the union pack. The success and viability of Wood Hood was tied to Blue's lumberyard. Granny didn't discuss much in terms of finances, but I knew from looking at her cupboards that things weren't going as well as they could. The union wolves were circling, and Granny couldn't stave off the pack alone.

I turned on the heel of my boot. "So how exactly could you *save* my Granny—if she were even to need saving."

"Why don't we stop and indulge in that delicious bakery treat you're carrying and I'll tell you all about it? I can smell the wonderfulness of chocolate and vanilla from here."

This guy could track down the Gingerbread Man by his nose alone.

"Won't you share your dessert with me?" His voice dripped with innocence, but I could swear I heard the undertone of deceit. "Please?"

In any other town than Amāre, if a total stranger asked for the food off someone's back the likelihood of that food being given was nominal. But in Amāre, sharing was a way of life. It was why Granny's Wood Hood had been embraced. The fact that this Mr. Wolfe had actually used "share," Granny and the town's buzzword, irked the hell out of me. Not to mention that he seemed to have the inside track on Blue's financial land holdings and in turn my Granny's wasn't helping.

"Oh ... all right." I wiggled off my backpack and unzipped it. The pink box somehow wasn't dented. I carefully held it and let my backpack fall to the ground. I tucked my lemon-printed skirt beneath my knees and knelt in a bed of soft moss that cushioned around me. I placed the pink box on my lap and gently peeled off the baker's golden seal of goodness that was taped over the lid. The triple-layer Neapolitan cake drenched in a thick layer of hardened chocolate wasn't munched either. *Oh, it's perfect.*

The subtle scent of strawberry, a hint of vanilla, and the rich decadence of chocolate wafted in the air. Suddenly my stomach grumbled—loudly. I looked up, and even though I didn't know this man, I was still a bit embarrassed. My belly sounded like a marching band had exploded into song.

"Yeah, I haven't eaten for a while either," I said and tried to think back to my last meal. A gourmet white cheese frittata at The Magic Oven. *Damn if Hansel isn't the best chef in town.* But that savory nosh was almost thirteen hours ago. In that time, I had photographed a bar fight at The Enchanted Forest tavern and the marriage proposal that ensued afterward. While I hated to admit it, stopping for a snack before hitting Granny's sounded like a good idea.

He knelt down beside me in the moss. "Thank you for sharing your dessert with me."

Like I had a choice? I nodded and reached into my backpack for anything that I could cut the cake. "Uh, I don't have silverware…" I dug deeper and checked into the crevices in my bag. "Not even napkins."

I looked up, and the man handed me a cloth handkerchief. "One problem averted." He reached into his pant pocket and handed me a closed Swiss army knife.

If he suddenly brandishes a sword, I'm not going to wait around to see if he's Bluebeard in disguise and has mistaken me for one of his wives. No thank you. I carefully took the knife and flicked open one of the blades. It was sharp to the touch. *Wonderful. I'm having dessert with a knife-wielding, deep voiced, big eyed, big handed, hairy stranger. Brilliant. At this rate, I'll never make it to Granny's house.*

Chapter Two

Why won't she get away from him? I tucked back behind the sequoia tree and watched them from a safe distance. *Run, little girl, run!* Though I knew from her long, tapered legs that stretched beneath her yellow skirt to the way her breasts strained against her gray hoodie, she wasn't a little girl. But when it came to Bernie Wolfe, no one was safe. Everyone was potential prey to be seized and devoured.

And right now Wolfe was weaving his magic on the beauty with the backpack full of bakery treats. Wisps of her hair fell like spirals from the hood of her jacket. Even without seeing her full mane of hair, I knew it was a bewitching shade of crimson. She had no business stopping in the middle of the forest with the hungriest animal in Amāre.

Think, Jack, think. I gripped the handle of my briefcase and shook my head. *Well this is useless.* Most men came into the Dark Forest armed with a hunting bow and arrow—anything to protect themselves from the wolves and other creatures that roamed at night. And even then, most men were ill-prepared for the predators. *Except that David kid who took down the giant with a slingshot. That was pretty badass. But, let's face it, that kid was a king among men.* My only weapon was my briefcase that was filled with ledgers and depository trust receipts for Giant Investment Services. It wouldn't bring down a pack of wolves, but it might bring down one wolf.

It was why I was in the forest. The Securities and Exchange Commission knew Wolfe was targeting elderly widows with retirement funds. *Hell, I alerted them to that little fact when Wolfe went after my grandmother and our bean crop. Bastard.* That's when the SEC recruited me to track down Wolfe. I possessed the one thing the SEC didn't have in its arsenal against Wolfe—a local connection to Amāre. I was born and raised in the merry little village, so I could be seen without being seen. It was why I was able to follow Wolfe and go undetected. It was almost too easy. I found him headed to Blue Ox's house, and I didn't have to eavesdrop to know the wily one was honing in on his next sizable asset.

If Blue actually handed over her portfolio to him, Wolfe could feasibly take control of her assets. *I can't let that happen—again.* Granted, my work with the SEC required that if Blue turned over her assets, that I get the transaction receipt to add to their case against Wolfe, I just couldn't see how I could consciously allow Blue to hand over her life's savings. It'd be the end of everything precious to her. I watched Wolfe mesmerize the young maiden in the forest with tales of saving Blue's holdings. *He doesn't save people, he destroys them.* There had to be a way where I could save the red-headed beauty before me and still destroy Wolfe. But how?

Chapter Three

"So your grandmother," he said. "She sounds like an amazing woman."

With a mouthful of Neapolitan cake and a stomach waiting for more, I nodded.

"I've never been very clear on how Wood Hood got started," he said.

I began to go into the spiel that I had written for all the Wood Hood marketing materials: local woman does right by lumberjacks, blah, blah, blah, but opted not to. Maybe it was the sugar fusing through my blood or the moonlight that made Mr. Wolfe suddenly seem less threatening. Whatever it was, I found myself telling him about the woman who helped raise me.

"When my granddaddy died, my Granny went back to work. She didn't want to sit idle. So Blue hired her, and Granny worked as a cook in the man camp at the lumberyard. Granny would listen to the men's conversations around the campfire and realized that the reason they weren't happy wasn't about money. In fact, they weren't asking for more money. What the men wanted was something to call their own." I inhaled the crisp night air. It was clean, fresh, and full of life.

"So anyway." I exhaled and felt cake in my stomach and the cool air around me. Together they settled my jumpy nerves. "Granny and Blue thought of ways that they could help the men feel like they had more ownership in their work. And actually it was Granny's idea to create the cooperative. She strove for everyone to share in the profit of their work. My Granny has the biggest heart."

"And because of Wood Hood she's got the second largest land stake in Amāre," he said matter-of-factly.

I shrugged. "Oh, Mr. Wolfe, that seems a bit of a stretch."

"Bernie. Please. Mr. Wolfe is my father. I'm simply Bernie."

"Well, Bernie, I know my Granny owns land in Amāre, but I don't know where she stands in numbers or how much land she actually owns. It's never really been something we've talked about. All I know is that she believes in sharing and for everyone's efforts to count."

Bernie's teeth gleaned. "So the cooperative strives for equality between the workers and the land owners, which in this case is Miss Ox."

I nodded. "Yup, Granny *and* Blue both believed that the lumberjacks and the owners should be treated equally in terms of pay and respect." I smiled. "I'm really proud of what the women accomplished."

Bernie slowly nodded. "It *is* something."

"So what do you do exactly?" I picked up the handkerchief of cake and took another bite.

"I'm a financial advisor and the owner of Giant Investment Services."

"And what do you do there?" The chocolate, strawberry, and vanilla blended sweetly in my mouth. "I mean besides being the owner."

He grinned. "Oh, what I do is actually boring compared to your grandmother's work. I simply help clients invest their savings into long-term securities."

"Have you always done that? Invest other people's money?"

He threw back his head and howled toward the moon. I think he was laughing, but I wasn't sure.

"Well, I began my career investing my own money. I started as a penny stock trader with money I had earned and saved when I peeled logs one summer for Pig Brothers Construction."

"Huh. I didn't know the Pig Brothers built log homes."

"They ended up going the brick route, but before that they were a stick and log company. Anyway." He fanned the air between us, and his musky scent made my nose twitch. "After I invested my money, I secured a loan with my father's Wall Street firm and set up Giant Investment Services. With the help of my father, who let me into his pack, my firm began trading on the stock exchange."

"Sounds fascinating," I said and meant it. "I can't imagine the hustle and bustle of Wall Street. Aren't you nervous? I mean you're trading someone else's money, right? What if you lose it all? Then what?"

"That's what sets Giant Investment Services apart. Initially we began on the stock exchange, but now we function as a third-market provider. So now we initiate orders from retail brokers."

"I have *no* idea what that means?"

He howled again. "Many people don't. It's complicated. But in a nutshell, we're one of the largest market makers on the NASDAQ. We invest wisely for our clients and don't take risks we wouldn't take with our own money. We grow our clients' money, and for someone like Miss Ox it provides a sense of security in an unsecure time."

When Bernie talked finances his dark eyes glistened and twinkled. There was a hunger to them that couldn't be ignored. *Granny could use a guy like this to oversee her finances.* "Sounds like you know what you're doing."

This time when he smiled, his fang teeth flashed. "I'm very good at what I do."

I wiped the corners of my mouth with the handkerchief and brushed the crumbs off my gray hoodie.

I packed the pink box back into my backpack beside the wine. "You should come with me to my Grandmother's house. I'd like to introduce you."

He licked his lips ravenously and smiled. "I thought you'd never ask. Show me the way."

Chapter Four

Oh, hell no. She is not taking Wolfe to her grandmother's house. It can't happen. Nothing good will come from this. It was bad enough that I probably couldn't save Blue from Wolfe. I knew when the SEC approached me to collect evidence that they needed one more widow and her assets to make a case against Wolfe and Giant Investment Services, but I just didn't think it would be Bunyan's widow. I glanced up at the tall, thick sequoias that Bunyan had climbed with a chainsaw effortlessly and easily. *I'm sorry, Paul. I promise I'll make this right—somehow.* Bunyan had given me the courage to take the rotten deal I got in a trade and make something good out of it.

Who knew some stupid beans would sprout into the largest bean crop this side of Idaho? But they did and before Bunyan died he was able to see how I had turned something sour into something sweet. Then Wolfe showed up on my Granny's doorstep, conned her into signing over her land claim and retirement fund, and that was the end.

Giant Investment Services seized our land and our crops and claimed Granny signed a "hold harmless" contract that removed their firm from any liability when their supposed investments went south. Granny was now living with that other little old lady and all her kids in a house not much bigger than a shoe.

It's just not right. The SEC would mostly have Blue to use against Wolfe. Blue would likely sign over her assets to Wolfe because he was so good at persuading widows that they needed him. But the SEC didn't need for this red-headed beauty to sacrifice her Granny, too. *Not if I can help it.*

I followed behind the red-headed beauty and Wolfe. I was just out of sight, but close enough that I could spring into action if I needed to. Again, I wasn't sure how much I could do armed with a briefcase, but luck was made from long shots.

Wolfe was closing in on red and her Granny's house. *Come on, Jack. Think, man, think.* I scanned my surroundings. Trees, trees, and more trees. I hid beneath one of the few weeping willows in the entire Dark Forest. Its limbs leaned over and touched the ground. They covered me completely. I reached up and tugged on one of the branches. It was bendable and sturdy. *Huh. If Tarzan could do it, I mean how hard could it be? The guy's in a loincloth. I've got on my Dockers.* I tucked my briefcase beside the trunk of the tree and grabbed the branch. I walked back and stretched the limb as far as it would go. *Yeah, this will totally work.* I looked around and found a boulder that was just within stretching distance. I backed up on the boulder and gripped the tree branch until it was taut. I waited until Wolfe and the fair-faced beauty were just within striking distance. I bent down and then popped off the boulder like a rocket. A rush of wind caught me at just the right time, or maybe not. I came through the willow like a human slingshot. *Uh-oh. Coming in hot.*

Wolfe seemed to sense me, or perhaps it was the blood-curdling scream that flew out of my mouth when I realized I hadn't quite figured out what I was going to do if Wolfe did the one thing that I hadn't factored into my plan: move. He stepped aside just as she looked up. Her eyes were a faint shade of green that seemed to darken as I approached. For certain her beautiful, expressive eyes widened in a mixture of shock and horror.

"What? Help!" She held up her hands, but it did nothing to cushion the fall that was inevitable.

I smacked into the red-headed beauty and hard. I landed on top of her and heard something crack. I wasn't sure if it was her bones or mine. Inches from her face, I gritted a smile. "Hey."

"Hey?" Her voice was on the cusp of panic. "Hey!" She pushed against my chest. "Get off me!"

I leaned over her and stared into eyes that were the color of the sweet, supple moss that covered the forest and grew up the sides of trees. Her eyes were just as soft in color and just as plentiful in their warmth. For a moment neither of us said anything. Her eyes darkened, and I couldn't tell if the shift in her mood was favorable or not. I decided not to press my luck. My growing attraction to her was already spinning far beyond the scope of what I was there to do. *This redhead was not part of the plan.* I pushed my palms against the ground to raise myself off her off when I spotted red seep out beneath her.

"Oh, no!" *Crap.* "I think you're hurt. Don't move!" I held my hand up, and I'm sure my eyes telegraphed all sorts of signals, none of which were favorable, romantic, or enticing. "Whatever you do," I said calmly. "Don't move."

She turned her head and saw the red liquid pouring out beneath her. "Is that blood?" She looked at me and then back to the seepage. "Is that blood!" She had now moved past panic and had entered hysteria.

I slowly nodded. "Could be." I looked around for Wolfe, but suddenly he had disappeared. I may not have been able to see him, but I knew he could be watching from the shadows.

I knelt down beside her. "Okay, give me a second. Let me think." But there wasn't time to think. A constant flow of red gushed out from beneath her. She needed medical attention. I scooped her up in my arms and cradled her against me. When I stood, she gasped.

"Are you okay?"

"You're so strong." The surprise caught in her voice and shone in her eyes.

I glanced into a face I could get lost into. "You barely weigh anything."

When she smiled, my feet felt lighter, my shoulders felt broader, and every worry I had faded from my mind. She was the only thing that mattered.

"Where are you taking me?" She looked up at me for answers.

"To your grandmother's house. I can assess your injuries there." Though I knew from how damp my arms were that things weren't good. I casually looked down at my forearms. They were streaked red. *Oh, no. No. No. No. Please don't die.*

She seemed to read me without having to exchange words. "Am I going to be okay?"

I picked up my pace, held her closer against my chest for warmth and walked with purpose. "You're going to be fine. Perfect. Good as new."

"Who are you? What's your name?" she asked.

I looked down at her. "Jack Hunter."

"I'm Scarlett Hood."

For a second, I paused. "Mildred Hood?"

She rolled her eyes. "That's my Granny's name, and while I was named after her everyone in my family calls me by my middle name—Scarlett."

"I know who you are. I just can't believe it's you. The last time I saw you, you were zipping around in that furry red jacket and beanie. You rode that John Deere around Pig's Construction yard like a boss. You and your Granny delivered lumber liked you owned the place. It was hilarious. Everyone on the crew called you 'little red riding Hood'."

Her cheeks tinged with color. "I was in my teens, and I was a bit of a rebel. I haven't been on a tracker in forever, and I *loved* that coat. I called it my gumdrop jacket because while you may have only seen red, it had these wonderful spots of color all over it—like gumdrops."

I smiled toward her. "Well, Scarlett it's nice to see you again."

She tilted her head, and long red spirals bounced out of her gray hoodie and fell against my arm. "So, Mr. Hunter, do you always fly through the night air and knock out unsuspecting women?"

I could feel heat rise from my neck up to my ears. "No." I curtly shook my head. "That was completely a first."

When she laughed it was deep, throaty, and sexy. She reached up and gently touched my face. "Thank you for making me laugh when I feel like I've just been run over by a truck."

"Least I could do. And I prefer to think of myself as a semi." I looked down at her and grinned. "A very large semi."

Her laughter echoed through the Dark Forest as we made our way to her grandmother's house.

Chapter Five

My Granny's house was lit by a single lantern that hung from the eaves of the wood porch. A slow, steady stream of smoke piped out of the red rock chimney that inched up the side of her house. I breathed a sigh of relief. *At least she's kept the fire going.*

"It's late. I should have been here hours ago," I said against Jack's chest. He held me tightly in his arms as he carefully made his way up the cobblestone path to the front door.

"Well, I'd rather bring you here in one piece than with that…" His voice trailed off.

"That what?" I looked around and suddenly realized Bernie Wolfe was not traveling with us. "Where'd he go?"

"Who?" Now his voice seemed to shift.

"This man who I was taking to my grandmother's house. Bernie Wolfe. He was going to help save my grandmother's finances."

Jack stopped just shy of the front door. He looked down at me. There was an intensity in his blue eyes that if I were to photograph I know would tell their own story.

"Listen," he said firmly. "I wish my grandmother had *never* met Bernie Wolfe. He's an awful beast, and he has no business meeting your grandmother. He lured in Blue. And he was setting you up for a trap."

"How do I know you're not doing the same thing?" My question clearly caught him off guard.

He stammered, and I held onto him tightly, afraid he might drop me. "I would *never* steal from someone's grandmother. Granted," he said. "I did take a few things from that giant of a man whose house practically sprouted up in the middle of my bean crop, but he had taken plenty from Amāre before his castle popped up on my land. But that's not the point. I'm *nothing* like Wolfe. I'm a local guy from Amāre trying to rid our merry little village from men like Wolfe and his pack."

"Is that why you crashed into me?"

"Let's get inside and see how you're doing first. Crashing into you was *not* my intention." He gingerly reached for the door handle. "I was actually aiming for Wolfe."

I tried to conceal my chuckle, but I couldn't. "Well, Mr. Hunter, you have awful aim."

"Admittedly, my aim was off," he sheepishly said. This time when he looked down at me I stared into the dark abyss of his eyes, and just like the aperture of my camera's lens, his blue eyes absorbed all the energy around him. In his gaze, he seemed to record everything. It felt timeless and beautiful to be lost in his focus.

"Scarlett, my intentions are pure and completely on target. I only want what's best for you and your grandmother. I would never intentionally hurt you."

As he laid me down on my grandmother's couch, I knew by his gentle touch and reassuring eyes that there wasn't another man in Amāre like Jack Hunter.

****

"Well, first off you're not dying." Granny was nothing if not pragmatic.

"But what about all of this…" I cautiously patted my side. "If I'm not dying what is this?" I held my red stained hand toward my grandmother.

She leaned toward my hand and sniffed. "Merlot? Or maybe it's a burgundy. Hard to tell with what you kids are drinking these days. It's some fruity-tutee wine."

I leaned my head back against the arm of her couch. "It's merlot." I looked up at Jack, whose color had all but drained from his face. "I was bringing wine and dessert to my Granny." I shrugged. "It's kind of our thing."

"No, our thing is dessert. The foo-foo wine is all yours," Granny said. "I'm more of a maple shots kind of drinker. Can't go wrong with something you can get straight from the tree."

Jack tentatively nodded, and his strawberry blond hair moved back and forth. "So I didn't break her? Or any bones?" He looked from Granny to me and then back to Granny.

Granny shook her shock of gray curls. "No sir, you probably knocked the wind out of her, and Scarlett's going to be sore from landing on a bottle of wine and breaking it, but no, you did not break my granddaughter. Hoods are built a lot stronger and sturdier than that."

Relief washed over his face, and color began to come back to his cheeks. "I'm so sorry. Your granddaughter was never my target."

Granny looked down at me. "I've got to go feed Blue's horses. I won't be gone long." She then glanced at Jack. "I trust you will help Scarlett get cleaned up?"

He nodded. "Absolutely."

Granny patted my knee. "Good. When I return I'd like to hear more about this Bernie Wolfe character you were both foaming at the mouth about when you came in and decided to stain my couch merlot."

Chapter Six

I clapped my hands together and practically scared Scarlett into a sitting position. "Okay, so I guess it's time we get you cleaned up."

She shook her head, and a mess of crimson spirals moved haphazardly across her fair face. "Oh, ouch." She reached up and touched the back of her head.

I was instantly at her side. "Lie back down." She gently slid on the couch. "Crap. Maybe you have a concussion." I looked behind me at the front door, but I knew Granny had already left. I carefully sat beside Scarlett and moved a wayward lock away from her face. I leaned over and started feeling behind the back of her head. I felt her eyes on me as I groped her head like I was checking a watermelon for freshness. I really wasn't sure what I was doing because suddenly touching Scarlett sent my senses into overload. Her hair was soft and silky between my fingers. I slowed down my rhythm and gently massaged her scalp. A low murmur escaped her lips. I quickly glanced at her, and her eyes were closed. I wanted to lean over and kiss her perfectly plump lips, but I returned my focus to her head where my hands wove through her wild hair that was a wonderland of richness. Even though she was soaked in wine, her head smelled like lavender. Now when I looked again at her, she looked up at me and smiled.

"I don't feel any bumps?" I asked as more of a question than a statement.

Scarlett's deep, husky laugh rose to my ears like an aphrodisiac that sent a signal to my brain and straight to my jeans as if she had suddenly cupped my cock. Her laughter was that enticing. It spiked a primal desire to have her beneath me with her mouth wrapped around my cock, which was beginning to grow as fast as my field of bean stocks.

I quickly shook my head and jerked away from her as if from a hot flame. "Yup," I said brushing my hands together and trying to shake free from the heat that radiated between us. "I think you're A-okay. Okay-dokay."

She looked up at me, and her faint green eyes questioned me. "What happened?"

I shrugged. "Nothing. Just taking Granny's orders to get you cleaned up. So let's get moving and get you ready." I hiked my thumb toward where I imagined the bathroom was located. "I'll start the shower, run a bath, or grab a bucket of water from the well." I scratched my head. "I'm not sure if there's running water out here. But no matter." I snapped. "I'll do whatever it takes." I pointed to Scarlett. "To get you freshened up." *Who am I?* I sounded like some jingle writer for a feminine hygiene commercial.

Scarlett shook her head. "But Granny won't be back for at least an hour."

I nodded. "Yes, but she left me in charge to get you cleaned up."

Scarlett slightly raised her hips off the couch, and her yellow skirt fell forward to reveal sheer panties that were streaked red. But even stained in wine, it was clear to see that Scarlett was a true redhead.

"I don't think I should move in my condition," she said with a coy look on her face. "Could you help me, Jack?"

I swallowed hard and looked at the tiniest, barely-there V-shaped panty that was held together by thin, pink, spaghetti-like straps that hugged Scarlett's narrow hips. I wanted to gnaw them off with my teeth to get to the strip of hair that was tucked beneath the sexy sheer. Instead, I held Scarlett in my gaze.

"Maybe you hit your head too hard?" I said trying to maintain some semblance of control, trying to be the good guy, trying to remember that we just met. Trying to get a handle on a situation that was suddenly moving too fast, too soon, and yet felt so right, which made no sense at all.

Scarlett rolled her head from side-to-side. Locks of her hair swayed in a truly mesmerizing, hypnotic fashion. "Jack, Jack, Jack. You over-think things way too much. If this Wolfe guy really is so bad and I really was in harm's way then you just came and rescued me." She looked up at me, and in that look I could have shot my load.

"Shouldn't we be living in the moment?" Her voice dripped with sex appeal, and my mind and body stopped working together. "Shouldn't we forget what's behind us and start moving forward? I'm not usually this way, but tonight hasn't gone *anywhere* like I had planned. I met some Wolfe in the woods. I knew he was bad news, I knew that, but I didn't listen to my gut."

For a moment anger flashed across her face. "I should have listened to my first instinct. But I didn't." She shook her head. "I did what was *expected* of me. I shared my dessert. I played nice."

Her hands were in her lap, and she opened them like she was releasing a bomb. "And then because of my kindness, I got knocked out by you, and now you tell me that Blue may have lost everything?" Her voice dropped like she was about to cry. "If we can't save what Blue lost…"

Scarlett placed both of her hands over her chest, and in that moment I could tell that what she needed. What she wanted wasn't necessarily me, but some retreat, some reprieve, some form of escapism from everything that had just happened. And if I could give her thirty minutes, though I hoped much longer, of total release, what was the harm?

"I didn't hit my head too hard," she said. "But I am having a difficult time getting up off this couch because I'm feeling a bit dizzy." Her tone started to shift. "So I was hoping that maybe you could help me?" She leaned on her elbows and partially unzipped her gray hoodie. "It's really wet and uncomfortable." She looked up at me, and I knew it was my last chance to give her something I'm sure she never asked for and never had to ask for. "Could you help me out of this?"

I knelt down in front of her while she lowered the rest of the zipper. Perfectly plum-shaped breasts, which strained against what was once a white, lacy bra that was now streaked with merlot, greeted me when I carefully reached for her arm. She turned toward me, and her left breast practically popped in my mouth.

She wiggled out of her hoodie and dropped it to the floor. "Are you good at unclasping a bra?"

I could no longer speak. My hands found their way behind her back that was caked with dried wine, and with a flick of my wrist her bra released in my hand. She slid out of it, and her breasts fell out of their constraints. I was there to cup them in my hand. My thumb circled her nipple until her back arched and low moans drew from deep within her. I circled the other nipple until I thought she would explode.

"Oh, Jack." Her head leaned back against the couch, and her nipples were erect with pleasure. I suckled on them volleying my attention back and forth just enough to tease and titillate without numbing the sensations. It was a fine balance and one that I prided myself on mastering. If this was our only moment together I wanted to savor every part of her succulent body. And her breasts were a magnificent feast.

I held one gently in my hand while I ran my tongue down her neck and around her rosy areola circling her fruit until she cried out for more.

"Jack!" She dug her hands in my hair while my tongue worked its way down her the curve of her body until it dipped toward her sheer panties. I moved my mouth toward the thin straps along her hips, and she arched to meet my tongue. I barely ran the tip of my tongue down the center of the sheer V-shaped material that separated me from her pleasure zone, and she screamed in agony. "Please, Jack, please."

But I never went beneath the panty. *Not yet.*

"Shhh." My tongue worked down her thong to her ass. I flipped her over and pulled her skirt up so my hands could roam her perfectly heart-shaped ass while my tongue separated her cheeks and licked sweet wine. The taste was an explosion of flavor in my mouth that was bitter, sweet, and tangy. I planned on savoring every drop of wine off her body.

Scarlett lay on her stomach, her crimson hair spilling down her back, groaning with pleasure. She was beautiful. I gently grazed her ass with my wet finger, and her head nodded.

"Yes. God, yes."

I slid my wet finger provocatively between her cheeks taunting the opening with the sensation of pressure, but never penetrating. I held onto her hips as if I was going to mount her at any moment. She moaned and arched her ass toward me.

But right when she thought the moment of ecstasy, the moment of release, was upon her, I moved away. I appeared in front of her at the base of the couch and pulled off my shirt. And with a snap of my wrist I unbuckled my belt and unzipped my jeans. I kept my fly open and watched her eyes widen as part of my cock poked through the opening.

I knelt toward her and touched the tip of my cock to her lips. She opened her mouth wide, but I pulled my cock away. She looked up at me. I moved toward her again and poked her mouth with the tip. She took a lick. I pulled away, and when I exposed more ridges of my rock-hard, expanded cock to her full mouth, she took a longer, more satisfying lick. I placed my hands on my hips and moved more and more of myself into her mouth in slow, deliberate strokes. I gave her as much of myself as I wanted when I wanted.

It didn't take Scarlett long to understand it was all about the tease and building up to the maximum payoff.

Scarlett leaned on her elbows. With her ass fully on display and her breasts hanging like ripe, succulent fruit I didn't stop her when she inched my jeans off my legs. I stood in front of her and decided what I wanted next. Her green eyes looked up at me. They were dark, and in their darkness I saw her curiosity and complete surrender. I stood at the base of the couch with my cock in her face. She gently nibbled on the tip, and then I placed the entire length of myself into her mouth. She coated it with her salvia that dripped down her chin. I gently pulled out of her and walked behind her and touched the wet tip of my cock against her round ass. She arched into me.

"Yes," she said.

I grabbed my jeans off the floor, reached into the back pocket and fished a condom out of my wallet. I tore off the wrapper, and the distinct scent of latex rose in the air between us. It wasn't a sexy smell like Scarlett's hair, but slipping the thin veneer over my shaft and watching my cock glisten as I stood in front of her heart-shaped ass, brought safe sex to a whole new level. There was something about Scarlett that I'd gladly wear a box full of rubbers if it meant being able to be with her again and give her this kind of pleasure.

I knelt between her knees and gently moved her thong aside and her cheeks apart. I leaned down and licked the opening. I moved the tip of my cock toward it, but not into it. She reached her hand beneath her and started rubbing herself.

I grabbed her hand. "Don't."

Her green eyes, now even darker, pleaded with me. "Please."

I shook my head. "Wait for it."

With my cockhead poking the opening of her ass and practically penetrating the seal, I reached around and grabbed one of her breasts and firmly squeezed her nipples. She cried out in pleasure.

"Jack!"

I moved my cock away from her ass and my finger took its place. I dove into her. She moaned as my finger pierced the opening. I fingered her while my cock stood at attention between her thighs. She raised her hips wanting me inside her, but I made her wait. I moved my cock between her thighs, but my finger moved faster.

I leaned over her and fingered her ass deep and hard while I rubbed her nipples. The combination drove her crazy. She ground against the couch until she screamed, and I felt her body constrict and orgasm.

She knelt on the couch, and I pulled aside the V-shaped panty and peered at the patch of strawberry-colored hair. I parted her thighs with my head and buried my mouth on her hot, creamy lips that oozed with cum. She gushed into my mouth. I tasted her richness inside me. Tangy, sweet, thick. I licked her tender, swollen lips and ate the bounty she presented before me.

"I want you," she said as her juices collected in my day-old scruffy beard.

I licked her lips and then licked up to her ass before taking my mount from behind her. My cock slid into her with force and intensity. Her lips clamped down on my cock.

"I'm going to milk your cock," she said with heated breath.

She tightened her hold and moved her pussy up and down against my cock like a fist. My mind shut off, and my body went into sensory overdrive. Her juices flowed down my balls onto my ass, and her muscles worked to milk my cock like it was ready for harvest.

She reached beneath me and stuck a wet finger up my ass while she milked my cock with her pussy. I felt a burst of cum shoot out of my cock. Not the full load, but enough to get my attention. She hit my erogenous zone, and it spiked my rhythm. I dove deeper into her pussy, and she dove her finger deeper into my ass. If there had been another person in the room I think we would have put his cock to good use. She fingered my ass, and I forged her pussy with my cock that had taken root deep inside her. Together we worked to milk my cock until it exploded.

We collapsed on the couch and turned on our sides. My hand cupped her breast and held her nipple, still wanting to play, but knowing that Granny would be home soon and that there was still a Wolfe lurking in the woods.

Chapter Seven

The cadence of his breathing against my back and his muscular arms wrapped tightly around me lulled me into a slumber I had not known. I could have slept for days. I felt safe in Jack's arms. It was as if I always belonged there and not as though I had just met him mere hours before.

I didn't fall asleep with shame or remorse from hooking up with a virtual stranger. Or for even coming on to him in the first place. It wasn't something I ever did, but as I lay in his arms with my ass pressed against his generous cock the only thought I had was when could we do it again?

But as I began to awaken, the feeling that stirred wasn't regret. It was not wanting this moment to end. I didn't want to leave Jack's arms. I didn't want to have to exchange pleasantries or engage in awkward "now what" conversations. And I don't think Jack would require any of those talks from me. It's why I just wanted to stayed tucked in his embrace. I wanted this one slice in time to be completely free from what was expected. I could be Scarlett, and Jack could be Jack. And together we could be ... *oh, what we could be together.* It boggled my mind and stirred my body.

But I knew my time in make-believe land was coming to a close. I knew Granny would be walking back from Blue's house and that she'd expect me to be changed. She'd expect a full report from Jack on Wolfe's whereabouts and what we planned to do next. She'd expect that I would have done what she had asked. What she wouldn't expect was for her granddaughter to be sprawled naked on her couch with Jack the bean farmer, now turned rogue SEC agent.

His lips grazed my neck, and I kept my eyes

closed, focused on the sensation of his mouth against me.

"You awake?"

I nodded, and tears stung my eyes.

"Maybe we should get you in that shower?" he said in the softest voice I have ever heard.

Again, I nodded.

He lightly swatted my ass and made me laugh when I most felt like crying, again if for no other reason than I had found a little sliver of happiness in the Dark Forest on the darkest night when I least expected it. And now I had no idea if this unencumbered, free-to-be-me, kind of happiness would find its way back into my life. It wasn't that I didn't have a good life. I just didn't have a Jack in my life. There were guys I dated. But there weren't any guys like Jack.

I rose off the couch and started toward Granny's bathroom when he called out after me.

"Don't go stealing all the hot water."

I gently looked over my bare shoulder at the man who had tried to knock out the bad guy and instead crashed into me and shook my head.

"I know how you Hood girls are," he said with a wry look in his eye. "First the hot water, next my heart."

I smiled and knew that there wouldn't be any awkward conversations or weirdness. Jack was a hero kind of guy. He wasn't your average hero by any means. But he was my kind of hero because he was flawed. He knew going after Wolfe was an impossible task. That the odds were stacked against him. Yet at every turn, I knew Jack would be the hero in his own story. And I was more than a little curious how this was going to end. I practically had a skip to my step when I headed toward the shower.

Chapter Eight

"So if Blue did sign over her land and stock portfolio to this Bernie Wolfe character then she's lost everything?" Granny asked.

Scarlett had emerged from the shower in what could only be described as virtual eye candy. She was in jeans, a barely there cream-colored peasant-like shirt that had strings that laced up the front and played peek-a-boo with her ample cleavage, which made paying attention to the conversation at hand a near impossibility. Still I tried because both Granny and Scarlett were intently staring at me.

"Wolfe's running the tried and true Pinocchio scheme." I smiled toward the two women whose curly hair and green eyes were a near perfect match. Though fortunately I would *never* confuse the two. Every taste and curve of Scarlett's body was forever seared in my memory. Now the red-headed beauty was looking at me.

"Pinocchio scheme? No idea what that means?" she said.

"Are you saying that Geppetto is behind all this?" Granny Hood slapped the edge of her kitchen table. "I knew there was something off about that little woodcarver. I mean any man that builds puppets for a living." She shook her head. "Not right, I'm telling you. Something's not right there."

I held up my hand. "No, no, Geppetto has nothing to do with this—only that this type of investment scheme is named after one of his wooden puppets."

"Are you sure about that?" Granny Hood really did not care for the puppet master.

Scarlet interjected, "Granny, you're talking about my Godfather."

Granny waved her away. "He's also the Godfather to an entire family."

I knew the inference. The Italian Geppetto was a puppet master in more than one sense. In the old country he was a mafia don. Since moving to Amāre he had retired his old ways and adopted the Amāre way of life—where sharing and caring went hand-in-hand. I gently smiled in Granny's direction. "I promise you. Geppetto has nothing to do with this. Let me explain it and hopefully it'll make sense." The two women nodded. "Okay, so Bernie Wolfe has been running a Pinocchio scheme where he uses newly acquired money, like Blue's holdings, to pay investment returns to previous investors. If he was a really good money manager and investor he wouldn't have to resort to a Pinocchio scheme to make up for all his terrible stock market buys." I glanced at Scarlett and Granny. They again nodded, so I continued. "Giant Investment Services is basically a dummy corporation—hence the name Pinocchio—that's about to fall like a house of cards. Wolfe has created a ton of dummy corporations that he uses to falsify and show profits from. But in reality these corporations are nothing more than make-believe. And like Pinocchio, Wolfe is prone to telling lies and fabricating stories for each and every investor he lures with his long tales of financial success."

Scarlett leaned back in her chair. "I believed him. I was taking him to meet my Granny."

Granny folded her hands in front of her on the table. "And Blue. My dear, sweet friend, this Wolfe has already darkened her door."

I grimly nodded. "Afraid so."

"Why couldn't you stop him?" Scarlett's tone was suddenly clipped and defensive.

"My work with the SEC is very clear. I was

brought on to track Wolfe and his activities and report them back to the field office. The SEC gave me a long rope, but not long enough to interfere until we had Wolfe in a position to make a case against him. And right now we don't have enough proof. So if Blue did or does invest with Wolfe, it's my job to get a copy of the depository trust receipt. That way the SEC will have proof that Wolfe is running a Pinocchio scheme."

"Don't they have other investors' receipts? Surely Blue isn't the first client that Wolfe has targeted." Granny studied me with green eyes that darkened and eyebrows that furrowed.

I exhaled. "Well that's the thing. I became suspicious when my Granny lost everything after she signed with Wolfe. That's when I notified the SEC. They looked into what my Granny had signed, and Wolfe had gotten smarter. He had her sign a 'hold harmless' claim that if his investments didn't pan out, my Granny couldn't hold Wolfe for any malfeasance."

"That's just not right," Granny said.

"It isn't. But since my Granny lost everything and then word started spreading in Amāre that she was penniless after we lost our bean crop and all our stocks, Wolfe upped his game."

"How?" Scarlett leaned forward in her chair. Her beauty was enough to take a man's breath away. She still had wet hair from the shower she had taken, and when I inhaled the subtle scent of lavender filled me with a renewed sense of purpose.

"And I'm sorry for snapping at you," she said and gently touched my hand. "It's just that when it comes to Granny and Blue I don't think clearly."

"I understand," I said. "So let me explain more about how this works because I *really do understand.* My Granny lost everything. And the how of it is that Giant

Investments Services always claimed to make huge profits for its investors, even during the Great Recession. But when a couple of investors saw what happened to my Granny they tried to cash out their investments." I paused because what I had to say next wasn't going to be easy to tell either of the Hood women. They seemed to sense my hesitation. Scarlett went from touching my hand to holding it.

"Whatever you have to say, you can trust us," she said with her hand cupped around mine.

I gently smiled. "I wouldn't be here if I didn't trust you or want what was best for you and your Granny." I squeezed her hand and then gently released it. I didn't want her to take it off with what I had to tell them. And her Granny might need her comfort more. "When a few investors tried to cash out their investments," I said, "they suddenly died under mysterious circumstances."

I could see in Granny's face the connection forming. "Woody Pig," she said, "One of the Pig Construction Brothers died when his house blew up supposedly by a gas leak."

"And his brother, Haley?" Scarlett said. "Didn't he die, too?

"Yes, I went to back-to-back funerals," Granny said.

"Haley Pig's house blew up when his propane barbeque exploded like a bomb," I said. "Two out of the three Pig Brothers died under mysterious circumstances after they both tried to cash out their investments with Giant Financial Services."

"Wolfe said he worked for the Pig Brothers and that's how he earned his start-up money. I can't believe he'd do that to the. What about the third Pig?" Scarlett asked.

"The eldest Pig never invested," I said. "He's also the one that took the company from a stick and log house builder to brick. He spotted Wolfe a mile away and stayed clear of him. But his brothers wouldn't listen to his advice and Wolfe blew their houses down—literally."

"And the SEC hasn't been able to tie this all back to Wolfe?" Scarlett said.

"Well, that's the thing. Until recently Wolfe has been very territorial and only targeted primarily elderly clients and particularly widows. He's had an affinity for the elderly. But when he went after the Pig Brothers that's where he tripped himself up."

"How?" Granny asked.

"Every investor with Giant Investment Services gets a free life insurance policy. The investors choose their beneficiaries, but in cases of accidental death, there's a hidden double indemnity clause that doubles the payout. The exception is that the other half of the payout goes to Bernie."

The women gasped.

"I know. So when the Pig Brothers both died, Wolfe doubled his profit on their life insurance payout."

"That's unbelievable. I can't believe he's getting away with this," Scarlett said. "There's got to be something we can do."

"The only thing we can do at this point is to either catch Wolfe in the act of trying to kill off one of his investors, which now that word has traveled in Amāre about the Pig Brothers, I doubt any investors will want to cash out. Or…"

"What?" Scarlett and Granny looked at me.

"We create our own Pinocchio scheme and dummy corporation that we get Wolfe to invest in. The SEC hasn't tied my hands so tightly that I couldn't pull this off," I said.

"Why would he invest when he does all these fake investments?" Scarlett said.

"Because he's greedy," Granny said. "And if he thinks there's a new stock that he can get in on the ground floor it'll buy him the time he needs while the SEC investigates him."

I nodded.

"Does he know the SEC is investigating him?" Scarlett asked.

"If he didn't, he did tonight." I shook my head. "I was trying to knock him out and buy time while I figured out my next move, but…"

"He saw you coming?" Granny said.

Scarlett laughed deeply and loudly. It made me smile and my cheeks tinge with heat at the same time. "Granny, it was kind of hard not to see Jack—he came barreling through the forest on a vine like he was on fire."

"Yeah, I hadn't expected Wolfe to see me and then when he did it was too late," I said.

"Then you might want to rethink screaming like Tarzan," Scarlett said.

"Point well taken." I could feel my ears burn with embarrassment. *At least she didn't realize I was screaming out of fear.*

"Okay so he saw you," Granny said. "But anyone in Amāre knows you're a bean farmer. How would Wolfe know you're with the SEC?"

I sat back in my chair. "That's a good point."

"Heck for all he knows, you were just some love-crazed man after my granddaughter's heart."

Maybe I am. I smiled inwardly, but outwardly rubbed the stubble on my chin. "So perhaps this could work after all. Wolfe *doesn't* know I'm working with the SEC or that I'm on to his little Pinocchio scheme. Unless he finds my briefcase." I grimaced. "Crud. That's still in the forest. I tucked it behind the willow tree."

"We'll go get it together," Scarlett said. "And unless your name is all over that briefcase, Wolfe still doesn't know what you were doing in the forest."

I nodded. "My name isn't on it. And it's locked. Not that he couldn't rip it open. That guy looked pretty cut."

Scarlett shook her head. "He's hairy and gross."

I chuckled. "So we get the briefcase and then…"

"Create a dummy corporation to lure him to us," Scarlett said.

She's sexy and smart. I nodded.

"But what corporation would get his attention?" she asked.

"The one I'm sure he's been trying to land for a long, long time," Granny said.

I looked at her and tilted my head. "The lumberyard?"

Gray curls shook toward me.

"The one his father, Wolfe Sr., sent our way," Granny said. "The one Bunyan fought off for years, but now that's dead, the pack keeps coming pack stronger and stronger."

I still couldn't connect the dots.

"The union," Scarlett said and kissed the top of her Granny's head. "Yes, of course. The union!"

I snapped my fingers. "Brilliant! That's the one entity that Wolfe would buy into. If we could create a dummy union that the lumberjacks have agreed to join, then Wolfe has everything he's ever wanted. He'd have the end of Wood Hood and Amāre would become Wolfe Town."

"Wolfe town?" Scarlett said with a touch of skepticism.

"Absolutely. If Wolfe becomes the largest land

owner by swallowing up Blue's assets whole and is able to add the lumberjacks to the mix there'd be nothing left of Amāre. He would have devoured it all. And for a man like Wolfe, there's nothing more satisfying than gobbling everything up," I said.

"So we'd better to get work," Scarlett said.

I exhaled a large sigh of relief. I hadn't broken little red riding hood when I came tumbling in trying to rescue her. And better yet now I was going to work beside the sexy, redheaded beauty to bring down one of Amāre's worst villains.

Chapter Nine

Finding Jack's briefcase was easy. It appeared untouched, and when he programmed in the key code, it opened and everything the SEC had on Wolfe was still safely tucked inside. But it wasn't enough to bring down the Wolfe of Wall Street. That's where Granny worked her magic. She assembled the lumberjacks together, and they awaited their instructions.

"They'd do anything for the queen of Wood Hood," I said to Jack who was by my side.

He stood stoically like he was about to address an army of wooden soldiers, and in a way he was. Jack was about to send them on a mission. My camera was slung over my shoulder. Jack and I had decided that if word didn't reach Wolfe, I'd post a few mock photos on the radio's website of the lumberjack's "unionizing".

"The lumberjacks are key, but having Geppetto involved is truly remarkable," Jack said with his focus on the men in front of him.

"Ah, that was nothing," I said.

He turned and looked at me with the zoom-like focus of a telephoto lens.

"What?" I said. "Do I have something in my hair?" I reached up and patted my spiral curls. "Because that happens all the time. My hair is a kind of magnet for birds, debris." I chuckled. "Anything that wants to land in it."

Jack gently reached out and tucked a curl behind my ear. His touch instantly relaxed me. My shoulders dropped, and I felt like I was floating on air.

"Your hair *is* a magnet," he said. "It's beautiful, but that's not why I was looking at you."

I couldn't do anything but smile when I was around Jack. Whether he was barreling through tree branches or carrying me in his arms to my Granny's house, he had a way about him that was remarkably heroic in the most unremarkable ways.

"Scarlett, what you did wasn't *nothing*. It was brilliant. No one else could have convinced Geppetto to get on board with our plan," he said.

"He wanted to protect me. I'm his goddaughter."

For a moment, I thought Jack was going to kiss me. He looked at my lips and even leaned toward me, but instead he repositioned my wayward curl that refused to behave.

"It's still amazing that Geppetto agreed to be the CEO of the fictional Wood Hood Union and let people think he's fallen back to his old mafia ways," Jack said.

"I know, right?" I shrugged. "He's so badass."

"Well, I did come up with that part of the plan," Jack said.

I grinned to stop from laughing. "Yes, you did. And what a plan it is." I elbowed him. "I came up with the photo gallery idea."

Jack playfully rolled his eyes. "Yeah, that's a good plan B."

I laughed.

Granny whistled at us from the side of the lumberyard. "We're ready when you are."

Jack quickly turned to me. "Make sure you don't get me in the photos. Only Geppetto and the lumberjacks."

I held up my thumb. "Yeah, got it. This ain't my first rodeo."

Heat rose to his cheeks. "Right." He clapped his hands together and raised an eyebrow. "Then, Scarlett Hood, let's get this party started!"

My spirits soared like a firecracker on the Fourth of July. This Jack Hunter was truly so different from any other man I had ever met in Amāre. I watched with pride as he took a giant step up onto the tree stump that Bunyan always used to address his men. While Jack looked small on the stump compared to how Bunyan had always looked, his voice was big and carried a message of hope.

"Gentlemen, thank you for joining us. I think together we can put an end to Giant Investment Services and save our merry little village of Amāre." He glanced over at Granny, who nodded.

Geppetto walked toward Jack and joined him on the stump. The two men shook hands before Jack continued to explain our plan.

I focused my camera on him and my lenses absorbed him. I couldn't seem to take my sights off him. I zoomed in on the lumberjacks, and he held their attention, too. I smiled. Jack wasn't their size. He couldn't do what they did. But they recognized a quality in him that I had—Jack exuded confidence. And that commanded respect.

"Geppetto has agreed to be the CEO of the fictional Wood Hood Union. He's doing this at the cost of his reputation. Everyone else in Amāre will believe that Geppetto has fallen back to his old mafia ways." Jack looked at my Godfather I'm sure for assurance. My Godfather gave him the head nod to proceed. "Geppetto wants it to be known around town that he wants someone else to run the operation so that he can concentrate on his puppet creations. We have to work together to get word back to Wolfe that Geppetto is willing to half what the union is worth if he gets an interested backer."

A rumble of murmurs spread across the men.

Jack held up his hand. "Remember this is all make-believe. None of this is true. We're out to capture Wolfe at his own game, but to do that, we all have to sell it as if it were true. So that's why we're having every lumberjack sign up to be part of Geppetto's union."

The rumblings died down.

"Once we gather the signatures we're going to head into town and The Enchanted Forest. The new bartender, Snow, was the last person to spot Wolfe. We think he's hiding out there in some sheepish attire to go undetected. So the plan is to go down to the tavern have some of the Bear Brothers' Honey Pot wine, or maple shots, or whatever you'd normally drink and while you're there, get talking." Jack paused and then smiled. "And get loud." He looked over at me, and I lowered the camera.

"I'll be wooing Scarlett at a corner table." He laughed at himself, and I felt my heart skip a beat. "The last time Wolfe saw Scarlett, I kind of crashed into them. I'm not the real Romeo type, so any tips you men may have I'm open to hearing."

A rowdy cheer erupted from the lumberjacks. "You can do this, Jack!"

"You tackled that giant bean stock, you can handle one date!"

I felt my cheeks burn with embarrassment, and an odd sense of pride filled me. Jack was claiming me as his own. No man had ever done that. Plenty of men had dated me, but none had ever had enough conviction or fortitude to actually court me, let alone tell a forest full of lumberjacks that they were going to woo me. *Jack, be nimble. Jack, be quick.*

Jack fanned down the crowd with his hands. "Okay, okay. I'll give it my hundred percent, and I need your hundred, too. Remember," he said. "We have to get word out that Geppetto is willing to let someone else run the union, but only in cash."

The men suddenly quieted down.

"This is key," Jack said. "We don't want Wolfe to offer Geppetto stock options in Giant Investment Services because it's a dummy corporation, so it's basically not worth the stock certificate it's printed on. We want Wolfe's cash—up front."

"How will this bring him down?" One of the lumberjacks yelled.

"We heard he already swindled Blue for all she's worth," another called out.

I looked over at my Granny. Blue had opted to stay at home.

Granny's voice suddenly rose above the men, Jack, and Geppetto. "I spoke to Blue early this morning. She fully supports our measures to bring this Wolfe to his knees. When she's feeling better she'll come down to the lumberyard to see each of you. She wanted me to pass on her apologies for placing you in this situation."

The men jeered. "Blue don't owe us no apology. She's our gal. We'd fight to the death for her."

"Well, that's sweet, and she knows how everyone feels. But she feels responsible for this mess. She allowed this Wolfe into her home and let him steal right out from beneath her. She's mad, but more than that she's sad. And I just hate to see my oldest and most dear friend so upset."

"No one messes with Bunyan's girl," a lumberjack called out.

"No one messes with Blue," another yelled. "Granny, you tell Blue we've got her six."

In the lumberyard, having someone's six was the equivalent to having their back.

Granny smiled, and I did, too.

"So getting Wolfe's cash. This will save Blue?" One of the men directed his question toward Jack.

Jack ran his fingers through his strawberry-blond hair, and it spiked in the center. "If we get Wolfe to liquidate everything he owns because he knows that…" Jack again looked at my Godfather, who again gave him the nod to continue. "Wolfe will know that a mob-controlled union is a cash cow. He'll use it as his personal ATM and reign supreme over Wolfe Town. So getting him to liquidate his possessions to have the cash to buy into Geppetto's union will save Blue and the entire town of Amāre."

The men pumped their fist in the air and together chanted, "Union! Union! Union!"

Their chant could be heard throughout the Dark Forest as they headed toward The Enchanted Forest tavern on the outskirts of town.

Chapter Ten

"I have not drunk. I have not slept." His hot breath was on my neck and sent shivers up my spine. I casually looked for Jack in the tavern, but he had headed to the men's room when Wolfe suddenly appeared behind me. "I have not drunk or slept out of anxiety, stress, and worry for you."

I turned toward him, and his fangs flashed from his ruby-colored lips. "My child, please tell me you're all right. I have been so concerned for your well-being."

In that moment, I had one of two choices. I could beat the Wolfe with my backpack that still reeked of merlot and Neapolitan cake and completely ruin our plan. Or I could stay the course and use my own cunning to seduce the wolf man. I opted for the latter.

"Oh, aren't you a sweet one." I gently reached up and stroked the side of his face. He hadn't shaved, and in just a day's time he had grown a full beard. It was no wonder none of the men recognized him. They were looking for a clean-shaven, three-piece suit wearing Wolfe. Not a bearded, flannel-wearing, lumberjack lookalike. *Clever disguise. If you wanted to hide something you hide it out in the open.*

"Whatever happened to you?" I feigned concern in my voice.

"I went for help." His dark eyes widened. "When that man came out of the woods, I knew that you must have been hurt so I went for help."

I nodded. "You are too kind."

"The better to assist you with, my dear."

I smiled. "Well, truth be told that man was actually trying to sweep me off my feet when he accidentally crashed into me." I giggled for good measure.

"Is that right?"

I nodded. "Yes, Jack's a sweet guy. I had complained that he wasn't being *romantic* enough and well…" I shrugged. "Go figure. Jack took that to heart and decided to swing into my life."

The Wolfe reached out and held my hand. "So you're all right then?"

"Perfectly fine."

"I'm so sorry I missed meeting your grandmother. I so much wanted to talk to her."

Tears instantly welled in my eyes. Maybe it was the thought that I had almost brought this beast to my Granny's house or maybe it was the idea of Granny losing everything like Blue—whatever caused the tears, it worked to my advantage.

"Oh, dear, why are you so upset?" Wolfe said.

"My Granny could have used you and your help, but now it's too late." I turned away from him and his foul breath. But again to Wolfe every action I took worked to my advantage.

"Please, dear child. It's not too late. I can still save your Granny from financial ruin," he said.

I shook my head and allowed my curls to roam across my face. "No, it is too late. The lumberjacks have unionized. There's no more Wood Hood to save. It's gone." I buried my head in the crook of my arm. "They unionized," I lamented.

"Unionized?" Wolfe's voice hissed toward my ear. "How is that?"

I looked up at him. "It's true. Geppetto got them to unionize."

"Geppetto?" Wolfe's dark eyes narrowed. "I thought he was a puppeteer."

I lowered my voice. "That's what he *supposedly* does. But he's the head of one of the largest Italian mobs."

"I knew he *had* ties with that Italian family," Wolfe said.

I chuckled. "Bernie, he *is* the Italian family."

"Really? I had no idea."

"You're probably the only person in Amāre who doesn't know that," I said with a touch of arrogance and conceit.

It worked because Wolfe's face tightened. "And he now has unionized the lumberjacks?"

"Yup. Geppetto *owns* the lumberjacks." I inched my finger toward Wolfe, who leaned in close. "And many of the guys didn't want to sign the union form, but when it comes to Geppetto 'no' isn't an option."

"So all the men are on board?"

"Oh, yeah. That's why Granny's lost everything. You could have saved her, but now—" I shrugged and let a long sigh pass before continuing. "No one can. She's penniless." My grandmother's financial position did nothing to interest Wolfe. *Jerk.* I looked toward the bar and spotted Jack. I slowly shook my head. *Stay where you're at. Do not come over.* He seemed to read my thoughts because he slid onto a bar stool beside one of the lumberjacks. I turned my attention back to Wolfe and put on my best game face. "And to top it all off, this Geppetto is already willing to let someone else run the union. Isn't it bad enough that he put my Granny out of business, but now he doesn't even want to run the operation? What kind of bull is that?"

Wolfe's focus narrowed until all I could see were the slits of his dark, beady eyes. "What is this? The don doesn't want to run the union?"

I shook my head. "What I heard from the men is

that he wants someone else to run the operation so he can concentrate on his puppet creations." I flung my hands in the air. "Puppets. What kind of shenanigans is that?"

"Did the men happen to say what he was looking for in a partnership?"

With my hands palm up, I rolled my shoulders. "Something like he's willing to give *half* of what the union is worth if he got an investor, but," I wagged my finger at Wolfe's long nose, "apparently only if they deal with cash. Doesn't that take all? *Cash.*" I paused just long enough for all of this to soak in. "But I guess it makes sense, doesn't it?"

Wolfe looked at me.

"He's the head of a mafia family. The only receipts he can show are the legitimate ones from his puppet business. He'd have to do the deal in cash." I waited for Wolfe to follow my breadcrumbs. "Right? I mean that makes sense doesn't it? A cash only transaction."

"Of course. It's the only way he could split the business."

"Yeah, but who in Amāre has that kind of coin?" I rolled my eyes. "Geppetto's got to realize he's not in Italy anymore. Cash. No one has that kind of cabbage." I traced the rim of my wine glass with my finger. I had to do something to stop from laughing. *Coin. Cabbage. I sound like a mafia princess.* "Oh well. Doesn't matter to me. I hope he ends up broke." I took a drink of my Honey Pot wine and turned back to Wolfe. "I'm probably not good company tonight, am I?"

When he smiled his fangs showed brightly. "Quite the contrary. You were delightful as always." He brushed his hairy hands onto his jeans and rose. "But I don't want to come between you and your budding romance."

I looked up just as Jack was approaching the

table. I smiled toward him.

"You're more than welcome to join us?" I said to Wolfe, who shook his head.

"No, I've got some business to attend to. It's been good talking to you again, Miss Hood."

I reached out and extended my hand. "Thank you for everything you were willing to do for me and my Granny. I'm so sorry it didn't work out."

"It was my pleasure." He gripped my hand, and I thought I was going to puke. "I hope you have a good rest of your evening."

Wolfe slid out of view just as quickly as he had entered. Jack sat down and raised his glass toward mine. "In case he's watching," he said.

"Oh, I'm sure he is."

"Then to catching a Wolfe." Jack leaned toward me with his glass, but before our glasses touched our lips did. An explosion of emotion erupted in that one kiss. I pulled away and looked into his blue eyes.

"Where did that come from?"

His smile was not toothy like Wolfe's, but rather soft, warm, and inviting like his lips. "We didn't really kiss the other night, and I've wanted to do that since I bumped into you."

"Bumped?" I said, laughing. "Are we still talking about your vine swinging abilities or your skills on my Granny's couch?"

His cheeks tinged in color. He answered me by leaning over and kissing me again. And again and again.

"So," Jack said in my ear. "Do you think Wolfe took the bait?"

I tilted my neck toward his mouth, and he nibbled just below my ear. I practically cooed a "yes."

Chapter Eleven

"So what do we do now?" I walked beside Jack toward his rust-colored pickup truck that was at the far end of the tavern's parking lot. Situated on the outskirts of Amāre, The Enchanted Forest tavern was a local hangout, but just beyond its reach was the Dark Forest. And even though I knew the way to my Granny's house, it had become one wooded area I wouldn't travel alone. Not anymore. Bernie Wolfe had changed that for me.

Jack turned on the heel of his cowboy boot and swooped in for another kiss. It was long, slow, and he lingered on my lips. "He could still be watching us. In fact, I'm almost certain he is," he said with his mouth pressed against mine.

"Uh-huh." I closed my eyes and let my lips wander across his.

"So I think we should stick together tonight."

I knew I should be concentrating on what Jack was saying, but my body was responding to his lips.

"Scarlett?"

I opened my eyes, and Jack's blue eyes shone in the moonlight. "Yes?"

He shook his head. "Your place or mine?"

"Right." I glanced toward the wooded forest. "Well, Granny's would be my place because *my* place is actually an apartment I share with my cousin, Rose Red. And she's always giving me lectures about talking to strangers and the inherent dangers of the Dark Forest. So I can *only imagine…*" I shook my head thinking of the mess and headache that would ensue trying to explain to my cousin Rose how I met Jack in the woods *after* sharing my dessert with Bernie Wolfe, yet another complete stranger. "Nope," I said. "I think my place is out. So we could go back to Granny's."

"Or we could go to my place," Jack said and unlocked the passenger door to his truck.

"Or we could go to your place." I stopped before getting into his truck. "And why are we doing this again?" The wine was definitely catching up with me.

Jack started to laugh and pushed back a strand of my wayward hair. He whispered softly in my ear. "To safeguard our cover in case Mr. Wolfe is watching you."

"That's right. So you're what?" I sat down on his truck. "My bodyguard, now?"

Jack handed me my seat belt and gently kissed my cheek. "I'll gladly guard your body. But this is about keeping you safe."

His blue eyes matched the faint sky that practically looked translucent with a bright moon glowing behind him. I almost wished Wolfe hadn't shown tonight because I didn't want my time with Jack to come to an end. "Thank you."

"My pleasure," he said before closing my door.
****

The drive into Amāre reminded me why it was the merriest little village on earth. Streetlamps burned brightly, and whether you lived in a cottage nestled on the mountainside or had a cookie-cutter type home in suburbia, Amāre wasn't just the town's namesake, it seemed a way of life. Everyone looked out for everyone. It didn't matter what car a person drove, or where they lived, it was what was in a person's heart that mattered. So someone like Bernie Wolfe didn't sit well with the townspeople of Amāre because greed wasn't a common core emotion. But love, love seemed to surround everyone and everything.

Jack pulled up to "Crossbow," an apartment complex that was on the corner of First and Arrow.

He cocked his head toward the upper level. "I'm on top," he said.

I sure hope so. I reached for the door handle, and a gust of wind practically blew it back shut. I giggled, and Jack hurried out of the truck.

"Let me get that," he said bracing the door against his side so I could get out.

I smiled. "Always coming to my rescue."

"Someone's got to." He held out his hand, and I slipped mine into his. It was a natural fit. I followed him up the stairs to his apartment. He unlocked the door, and an orange tabby sashayed across the carpet as if to announce that we had entered her abode.

"Pumpkin!" Jack said.

I knelt down, but the tabby tilted her chin high in the air and sauntered off with the arrogance and conceit of a well-groomed feline.

"Wow." I watched the cat stroll across the carpet before she slipped into the next room. I turned to Jack. "I've *got* to learn that move."

"Yeah, Pumpkin's got it going on. She's wicked sassy. No one messes with Pumpkin."

"No kidding." I shook my head. "If I had half her moxie."

Jack chuckled. "You held your own tonight with Mr. Wolfe."

I rolled my eyes. "That remains to be seen."

"Don't underestimate yourself, Scarlett. When you want something, you're pretty convincing."

I looked up at him and felt my cheeks tinge with heat. Still for good measure I played along. "Is that right?"

Now Jack's cheeks grew rosy and bright. "Yeah. I can't imagine *any* man not giving you what you want *or* not believing whatever story you told them."

I steadied him in my sights. "I wasn't playing you, Jack."

Jack placed his hands on his hips as if taking a stance. "I don't get played."

"Good." I pivoted on the heel of my boot and tried to make a fancy exit like Pumpkin, only my heel slipped on the carpeting and I started to tumble like a house of cards. Jack reached out and caught me just before I fell onto his glass end table.

I landed softly in his arms and covered my face with my hands where I started laughing. "Yeah, I *so* wasn't playing you because my best moves usually end up like this."

He leaned over me and kissed me. His tongue explored my mouth and moved down the nape of my neck. *My God, this man's tongue is a national treasure.*

I leaned back in his arms and felt like I was floating on air. He laid me down on the thick carpet, and my body was cushioned on velvety warmth. He began to untie my blouse that seemed to unravel like a maze of strings in his hands. I looked up at him. "Do you want some help?"

His blue eyes focused in on me while he considered my offer. He slowly rubbed the stubble on his chin. "I'm not sure I want this off." He reached his hand into my blouse and unhooked my bra. He slid it off, tossed it aside, and my breasts bounced free beneath the sheer material.

He raised an eyebrow. "Much better." He thumbed my nipples through the outside of my blouse until they stood at attention and practically poked through the material. I looked down, and even I was turned on by the utter visual he had created by simply removing my bra. My dark nipples and large, round areolas were fully, erectly on display. And when I looked down at his jeans so was he.

I sat up and playfully, very carefully, put the tip of my boot toward his growing boner. "Jack, be nimble, Jack, be quick."

"Wrong Jack," he said grabbing my boot and pulling it off my foot. "He's much shorter than me. And not nearly as nimble as you'd think."

I grinned while he reached for my other boot, hefted if off and tossed it over his shoulder. He pulled the frayed ends of my jeans and yanked me closer to him. With my legs spread apart and Jack sandwiched between them he began to unbutton my jeans. My body temperature spiked. He slowly lowered the zipper, and already I was slick with moisture. *Never before has a man turned me on simply by touching me.*

My heart pounded, and my skin tingled with anticipation. He began to lower my jeans off my hips when without any warning he stopped and abruptly stood.

I shook my head. "What?"

He stood above me. "I just realized we haven't eaten."

"I thought you were about to?"

He chuckled. "Aren't you hungry, Scarlett?"

I curtly shook my head. "Nope." I pointed down to where he had been. "I think this was satisfying whatever craving I was having."

When Jack smiled it only magnified my want for him. He held out his hand. "We should eat."

"No," I said in as adamant a tone as I could muster with my jeans open and feeling extremely wet and wanton. "Eating is *not* what we should be doing right now."

But Jack didn't change his position. He stood above me steadfast with his hands on his hips. *What the hell?* I was about to zip up my jeans and grab my bra and boots when I noticed that while he hadn't changed his position about food, his boner also hadn't changed its position either. If anything it had gotten larger. *Ah, Jack.*

He just needed a little convincing. I looked at his cock that had shot up in his jeans like a beanstalk. The man that had conquered so many giants in his life and was about to conquer yet another one tomorrow had a lot on his mind. I barely knew Jack Hunter, but I knew he was one man that needed to feel as though he was calling the shots. I knew he wanted to be with me. Not because his cock was telling me, but because his eyes were.

"You're right," I said slowly rising, but instead of standing I knelt before him. With the pretense of zipping my jeans, I let my blouse fall forward so that it dipped and revealed my breasts without letting them show entirely. *I want you as much as you want me.*

I looked up at him and started to zip up my jeans. "You know what, we *should* eat." I was eye level with his bulge. "I haven't had *any* protein today." I drew a deep breath and let my breasts rise and slowly fall. "What sounds good?" I glanced down at my jeans and let my hair shield my face while I purposefully fumbled with my zipper.

"Oh crap!" I dramatically threw my head back and closed my eyes in feigned defeat.

"What?"

"Ugh! I think I broke my zipper." I shook my head and exhaled. When I opened my eyes Jack was staring at me. My blouse was falling off my shoulders, my breasts were on display, and my jeans now exposed more of my very naughty, red, lace panties that I had worn specifically in hopes that Jack would find his way into me again. The big reveal was that the panty was crotch-less. But to get to that reveal was going to take some doing.

"Oh, well." I exhaled and let my breasts heave. "Do you have some sweats or something I could borrow?"

Jack nodded. "Uh, yeah."

"Great." I popped up as quickly and unexpectedly as he had done to me and my breasts bounced along with me. I shimmied out of my jeans like I wasn't trying to turn him on—again. Next, I made sure I picked up my jeans with my foot and slightly kick them away from me. My kick was deliberate so that even a blind man would know my panties were crotch-less because when I lifted my leg the sweet scent of a hot, wet, wanton woman wafted between us. There was no denying that I was turned on, and by the wide-eyed look on Jack's face there was no way he had either.

"So those sweats?" I looked at Jack.

He grabbed my wrist and pulled me into him. His cock pressed hard against me. Heat coursed between us, and I could barely catch my breath.

"I don't think you should ever wear clothes," he said.

But I quickly regained my composure. With my free hand I swatted his chest. "Oh, Jack," I said, rolling my eyes for good measure. "Come on."

With Jack still holding onto me, I slightly turned toward the kitchen and exposed the luscious, seductive, red satin thong that hugged my ass and screamed for his cock to ride up against it. "Let's go eat."

His hold on me grew stronger. I looked back at him. "What? Aren't we going to make something?"

He shook his head.

"You want to go out and grab a bite?" I glanced toward the front door. "I bet The Magic Oven's still serving. Oh," I said with feigned enthusiasm. "We could go pick up one of their take and bake pizzas. That Hansel knows his way around some dough. And his sister Gretel's no slacker when it comes to desserts."

Jack's eyes zoomed in on me, and it was hard to tell if he was on the verge of laughing at me or loving on me. I wasn't sure. I just knew that I hated to see him torn between what he wanted to do and what he felt he should do. I knew he wanted to be with me, but I knew he felt a sense of duty to do what was right. Right by my Granny. Right by Blue. Right by the lumberjacks that had entrusted him and pretended to unionize. Right by Geppetto, my Godfather. Right by the SEC. And right by the town of Amāre.

I didn't want to be one more person placing a demand on him. Or someone he felt he had to do "right" by. Yet he still held onto my wrist. He wouldn't let go. I don't think he knew how. I walked back into him. No games. No teasing. No taunting. I reached up with my free hand and gently touched the side of his face.

"Whatever you decide to do tonight. I just want to spend it beside you," I said.

Relief washed over him. Tension fell from his forehead, the lines around his eyes softened, and his jaw relaxed. And the way he pulled me into him was like coming home. I leaned against his chest, and he gently kissed the top of my head. *I could spend forever right here.*

"I just have one question," he said quietly in my ear.

I looked up at him.

"Where in Amāre do you get your panties?"

Our laughter mixed together, and it was the sweetest sound I had heard since this whole Wolfe thing started. Jack scooped me up in his arms like he had in the

Dark Forest and carried me into his bedroom. A silvery moon cast its light on his bed. He laid me down and propped me against his stack of pillows. I had a bird's eye view of Amāre that no postcard had ever captured. It was breathtaking, but not nearly as captivating as watching Jack as he peeled away his shirt, kicked off his boots, or stepped out of his jeans to make his own reveal. *Commando.* I widely smiled. *Nice.*

Standing in the moonlight, firm chest, muscular arms, toned legs, he looked like a Greek god, and I wanted to worship at the altar. *Damn.*

I slipped off my blouse and crawled to the edge of the bed before him in my red, lacy, satin, barely-there panty and nothing else. I looked up at him, and if I could make a promise with my eyes it was that tonight would be memorable.

He raised an eyebrow and smiled back. His cock seemed to be making the same promise. I put my hand under the ridge of his cock, just below the tip, and started to stroke it. His body responded immediately. His cock jutted toward my mouth, but I kept my lips sealed. I stroked the head without going down the full shaft of his cock, and it drove him crazy. The tip of his cock oozed with drops of cum. I looked up at him and took a long, slow lick.

He tasted tangy and bitter. His scent was a mixture of musky and sweet, sweaty and clean. Everything about Jack was a contradiction. He was strong and yet vulnerable. He was fearless and reckless. He'd fearlessly swing in to save the day, only to recklessly miss the intended target. In public he watched his Ps and Qs, but privately his proclivities ran prolific. He was all man.

And just as soon as I thought I was in control and had him where I wanted him, Jack flipped me on my back and ran his hands down my torso. The weight of his body pressed against me with his cock directing his every move. I reached down between his legs and cupped his balls.

He dug his mouth into my shoulder and I arched toward him, but I knew Jack. I knew he would take his time and that I would enjoy every minute of delayed pleasure. His tongue roved my body moving from my breasts to my belly button but never settling on one place very long. His movements were quick and sporadic and drove me crazy. I raised my hips toward him, and he reached into his nightstand and pulled out a condom.

I watched as he tore the package open with his mouth, and I practically salivated, knowing what was coming next. He slid it down over his cock. Jack entered me from the missionary position, but then he slid to his side and draped my legs over him. We were like one giant "X" on his bed.

Suddenly I felt more of his body in motion with mine. I reached around and grabbed his ass as he thrust into me. I pulled him deeper and deeper into me. With one hand on his ass and my other hand wrapped around his shoulder, I dictated each thrust. I brought him further into me with greater impact and force. I controlled his cock.

He reached down between my legs, which were drenched with sweat, and began to rub my wet clitoris. I thought I would stop breathing. My body was already close to orgasm, but with Jack's hand on my clit combined with my hand on his ass, moving his rock-hard cock in and out of me, the entire thing tilted my vanilla world on its axis. My legs clamped down on him, my back arched, and for a moment I think I lost consciousness. For certain, I know I purred as my claws dug into him. Pumpkin may have her moves, but so did I.

PUMPKIN SPICE

Chapter Twelve

My phone buzzed with an incoming text. It was from the SEC. I quickly read the message. Wolfe had made contact with Geppetto. Now, it was my turn. I had to deal with one of Amāre's worst villains. I slipped out of bed and into my clothes. I didn't look back at Scarlett. I couldn't. I grabbed what I needed and left. No note. No explanation. No loose ends.

Before I showed up for the designated meet, I had one last stop to make.

It seemed like there were more shadows in the Dark Forest or maybe it was my mind playing tricks on me. I tucked my chin in the neck of my jacket and braved the cold that had woven its way into the air like an unwanted guest. Smoke rose from her chimney. I gently knocked on her door. Dawn hadn't even broken when she opened the door.

"Jack? Is everything okay?"

I nodded. "May I come in?"

She stepped aside, and I walked in.

****

I left her house through the back door and glanced in either direction before heading toward a back road I didn't even know existed. It would get me out of the Dark Forest and back into town almost undetected. I patted my jacket pocket. The most important part of my day was still safely tucked inside. It was only a matter of time before Wolfe got was coming to him and so did Scarlett.

Chapter Thirteen

Her tail brushed across my face and tickled my nose. I ducked under the blankets, but I knew she was as persistent as she was proud. She wouldn't stop until she had nothing short of my complete attention.

"Hello, Pumpkin." I pulled back the blankets and looked at her. She turned her head as if I hadn't spoken. As if I were a nuisance in her morning routine.

I literally gasped. "Oh, you cheeky, little thing." I turned on my side, yanked the comforter that the tabby was curled up on, and she tumbled to the floor with a small yelp. I looked over the side of the bed, and her green eyes looked up at me in complete disbelief. "Uh-huh. Well, I didn't mean for you to fall *off* the bed."

I patted the pillow where Jack had slept and I had fallen to sleep on his shoulder, and in one swift motion Pumpkin was up on the bed and back beside me. I turned toward her. "So where is he?"

Pumpkin didn't turn away when I spoke, but she didn't answer either.

I exhaled. "Yeah, I'm not sure either." I picked up my cell phone off the nightstand. No missed calls, text messages or voicemail. *Hmm.*

"Maybe he's the love 'em and leave 'em kind," I said to the orange-and-white striped cat that looked like it had been tie-dyed. "Although..." I looked around his room. "Usually they don't leave when it's their place and I'm still wearing his clothes."

I sat up in bed, and Jack's navy-colored t-shirt bunched around me. It was two-times too large and a perfect fit. It was soft, worn, and made for the best after-sex attire. I fingered my hair back into a ponytail and then twisted the ponytail until it was one long twist of hair. I wrapped the twist clockwise around my head into a messy bun that I tucked into place with a loose curl that pulled it all together.

"Voila!" I tilted my head toward Pumpkin whose interest I had actually garnered. *Go figure.*

My cell phone chimed. "Maybe that's Jack!"

A text message appeared across the screen from a number I didn't recognize. "Come to the Old Lumberyard offices at 5 PM."

"Well, that's interesting." It was ten in the morning. Five seemed like a really long time to wait to find out who had asked me to a meeting at an office building that hadn't been occupied since Paul Bunyan died.

I looked at Pumpkin. "I think it's time to go visit an old friend."

****

"Sometimes you ask too many questions."

"I'd have to agree."

I looked from my Granny to Blue and then back to Blue. "What?" I placed my glass of iced tea back on its coaster on the kitchen table in Blue's house and noticed that neither Granny nor Blue were drinking tea. "Is that Maple? Are you drinking maple shots?" I glanced at my watch. "It's barely noon."

Granny spoke first. "Like I've always said, 'You can't go wrong with something you get straight from the tree.'"

I shook my head, and my bun practically fell from its perched position. "Okay, so maybe it's the maple shots talking because I don't think either of you heard me correctly. I got an anonymous text to meet someone at the Old Lumberyard offices." I raised my shoulders. "It could be Bernie Wolfe for all I know. Or that little trickster Rumplestiltskin. He's always spinning something."

Both women waved their hands at me as if I were

a bothersome fly. "Scarlett, your imagination is wild."

"No," I shook my head. "My imagination is not wild." *Well, actually since meeting Jack...*I quickly regrouped. "Listen, ladies, someone is using Paul's old office, for what, we don't know. I think we should contact the Amāre police."

I held out my cell phone, and both women practically leaped across Blue's oak table to grab it from me. And that's when I knew something was amiss in Amāre. I tucked my cell phone into my gray hoodie, reached for my Granny's glass, and in one swift move threw back the sweet, maple-flavored whiskey that hit the back of my throat with a hint of smokiness and a rich note of honey.

I looked at my Granny and her oldest friend, who looked at me with wide eyes and painted on smiles. "Would you like some more, dear?" Granny asked. "Blue's got a whole bottle of the stuff. It might settle your nerves."

I held up my finger. "Don't."

"You do seem a bit jumpy," Blue said.

I wagged my finger at the seventy-year-olds who acted as though diving across tables was a common occurrence for them.

"Nuh-uh. Not a chance," I said. "Start talking. What gives?"

But neither of them would spill the beans.

I looked at them. "Is this about Jack?" There was a drop in my voice that couldn't be masked. I knew that Jack's next order of business was Bernie Wolfe. I didn't know where or when or how.

"All I'm going to say," Granny finally said, "is that the bun on your head is not very becoming. Not at all."

What?

"I'd have to agree," Blue said. "The Hood women have beautiful red hair."

"Scarlett, you really should go home, take a shower, a very long shower, shave, wash your face, put on some makeup, a dress, and then go make this appointment at five," Granny said. She pushed out her chair and walked over to me. "Sometimes," she said softly in my ear, "happily ever after isn't just for fairytales."

Chapter Fourteen

At exactly the stroke of five, I heard her boots against the wood-planked staircase outside the office. I smiled. *She's on time.*

The door to the office was already open, but I stepped out onto the threshold to meet her.

"Jack?" Her eyes questioned me.

"Who were you expecting?"

She raised her shoulders, and crimson spirals bounced against her jean jacket. "I wasn't sure what to expect."

"I was trying to be mysterious," I said.

She slowly nodded. "Well, you were that."

"Are you okay?"

It took her a moment to answer. "Why am I here?"

I reached for her hand, but she held it at her side.

"Scarlett, I wanted to share this with you."

"Share what?"

I extended my hand toward the office. "Welcome to 'Wood Hood Union'."

The name had recently been stenciled on the exterior office door. Scarlett touched the lettering as she walked inside. Her white skirt kicked up beneath her with each step.

"This used to be Paul's office," she said.

"Yes, and today it was where Mr. Wolfe met his match." I led Scarlett into the room where an open briefcase sat on the edge of the desk.

"Oh, my gosh!" She walked directly to it. "I don't think I've ever seen that much money in my life!" Her green eyes were wide and suddenly filled with wonder.

"It *is* a lot of money." Beside the open briefcase, two other cases were equally as full. "And the best news?" I said.

She continued to look at me for answers.

"It's all going back to every single person Bernie Wolfe ever defrauded." A sense of pride filled me. "My Granny will no longer have to live with that lady and her kids in that shoe-box of a house."

"So Blue will get all her hard-earned money back, too?"

"Absolutely," I said. "Everyone who was a victim of Wolfe's Pinocchio scheme will be given back what he took from them."

"So how did it all go down?" Scarlett asked. "I know that the SEC wouldn't allow me to be part of it for safety reasons. But I didn't know what was happening or really when. You weren't there this morning, so I just…" Her voice trailed off, and I realized that maybe what I had set in motion wasn't going as well as I had hoped. Or planned.

"I wish you could have been there," I said.

She softly smiled. "I understand. It's just kind of been a weird day. First the text, then my Granny and Blue, now this…" She shook her head.

I reached into my pocket and withdrew my cell phone. "Since I couldn't tell you what was going on and I did kind of lead you on your own wild goose chase, maybe I could make up for it now?"

She looked at me.

"How'd you like to watch it on video?"

She lightly whacked me on the shoulder. "Seriously?"

"Oh, yeah. I may have recorded the entire thing so that I could show it to you later. You know I couldn't have done any of this without you, your Granny, Geppetto, and the lumberjacks." I paused. "But really *none* of it would have happened without you, Scarlett.

You set the trap, and Wolfe walked right into it."

When Scarlett smiled at me, the world stood still and time stopped.

"So you want to see it?" I waved the phone toward her.

"Yes!"

Her mood completely changed, and I felt like I had set right any wrongs my absence and silence had created.

"Okay, I'm not a photojournalist like you," I said and shut the briefcase full of money and moved it to the corner of the desk. I patted the top of the desk, and Scarlett sat on it beside me. "But I couldn't let this moment pass without you being part of it." She leaned her head on my shoulder.

"Ahh. So you secretly recorded it for me?"

I nodded. "I did. And it goes completely against SEC protocol, so it's our little secret." I slid open the video recorder on my phone, and Bernie Wolfe came into view. He stood outside the office door that Scarlett had just walked through.

I watched Scarlett as the video played of Wolfe walking into the empty office.

"What?" Wolfe said. "Where is everyone?"

From the corner of the frame, I stepped into view. "Hello, Bernie."

"Tarzan boy? What are you doing here?"

Scarlett paused the recording. "Tarzan boy, huh?"

I shook my head. "He's an idiot. Everyone knows Tarzan only wears a loincloth, and I wear Dockers."

Scarlett shrugged. "Bummer. I'd bet you'd look amazing in loin anything."

"Later." I grinned. "Now watch the video."

She resumed the playback mode.

"Bernie Wolfe, I'm Jack Hunter with the

Securities and Exchange Commission," I said on film, and Scarlett clapped.

"The SEC? No. You're a just a poor bean farmer."

I shook my head. "Yeah, and you're just an honest financial investment advisor."

"What is this? Where is Geppetto? Where is my union?" Bernie looked frantically around the empty office.

"Well, that's the thing. There is no Wood Hood Union, and Geppetto's in his shop making a new wooden puppet he's calling 'The Lone Wolfe'."

"What? How can that be? I paid Geppetto cash. We had a cash deal."

I shrugged. "I'm not sure about any cash transaction. But you could always file a complaint with the SEC that you've been a victim of fraud."

Scarlett cheered and clapped her hands together. "Yes! Way to go, Jack!"

I grinned. "Just wait. The best is coming up."

Wolfe tilted his head toward the ceiling and howled in disbelief. He had liquidated his house, his holdings, and all his offshore accounts. His howls of destitution reverberated through the empty building and echoed across Amāre.

"Is that what I heard today when I was in the shower?" Scarlett looked at me. "I thought an animal died."

"Well, one did. When Wolfe realized he was flat broke and couldn't complain to the SEC that he was the victim of the same fraud that he'd perpetuated on others, I'm sure a part of him did die." I nodded toward the phone. "There's just a little more to watch."

"I want my money back!" Wolfe lunged at me on tape, and I stood my ground.

"Mr. Wolfe, I will gladly file your claim with the

SEC. First I will need the depository trust receipt you were given from Geppetto. This will allow the SEC to file charges against one of Amāre's largest crime family syndicates. We'd be more than happy to comply and get those proceedings started."

"But my Godfather isn't in the mob," Scarlett said. "He's an honest businessman. He really *is* a puppeteer."

"Ah, yes, well *we* know that, but Bernie doesn't."

Scarlett's face lit up like a firecracker. "Brilliant!"

"So," my voice played back on the recording. "If you could provide the SEC with all your financial interactions with Geppetto, we'd love to bring down the Godfather of the Amāre mob."

"No, no. I have no complaints to file against Mr. Geppetto." Wolfe shook his head, and his normally perfectly coiffed black hair suddenly seemed unkempt and scruffy.

"He's a mess," Scarlett said.

"Fraud, right? It'll screw you up every time."

Scarlett turned her attention back to the video.

"Well, Mr. Wolfe, you could always go after Geppetto yourself, though…"

"Oh, you let your voice trail off purposefully didn't you?" Scarlett practically gushed.

"Perhaps…"

She elbowed me. "Cute. That's cute."

I tapped my phone. "I think *this* is my favorite part."

Wolfe combed his fingers through his hair, and he looked wildly at me like a crazed, trapped animal.

"Mr. Wolfe, since you'd rather not file a complaint with the SEC and you don't want to go after Geppetto yourself, I'd leave Amāre and never come back, if I were you. If you stick around you may have an accident, and if it's fatal, Geppetto collects double."

Color drained from Wolfe's face, and he ran from the room.

Scarlett erupted into cheers and applause. "Yes! You did it! You nailed him! You got the Wolfe of Wall Street!"

I turned off the recording and tucked my phone back into my pocket. "Scarlett, *we* nailed him."

"Only after you nailed me first in the Dark Forest," she said. "Or was that actually on my Granny's couch…"

I shook my head. "You're looking at it all wrong. I *swooped* into your life."

"And if you hadn't I would have been at the end of my rope," she said with her hand on her chest, and her head tilted back like a classic damsel in distress. "Oh, Jack," she said playfully, "I would have been left to deal with the big, bad Wolfe all by myself."

"I would never have let that happen." I jumped off the desk, dropped to one knee and withdrew the velvet box tucked in my other coat pocket.

Scarlett gasped.

"I grabbed that vine and came crashing into your life for a reason," I said.

Tears suddenly pulled at the corners of her green eyes, and her lips started to tremble.

"And ever since I did, Scarlett, ever since I met you and have been with you, it's where I want to be." I held the box tightly in my hand. "But I know that family means everything to you."

She nodded as tears fell from her fair face.

"So this morning, before Wolfe, before the SEC, before anything else, I went and asked for your Granny's blessing."

Scarlett's mouth formed a perfect O.

I smiled. "I did, and your Granny's one wise woman. She said she knew we were meant for each other. That her granddaughter had found her—" I paused. "How did she say it?"

"Happily ever after," Scarlett said softly.

On bended knee, I looked up at my green-eyed, red-headed beauty and smiled. "That's it. She told me that by the way we looked at each other when I brought you into her house that we had found our happily ever after. She knew by a look."

Scarlett smiled.

"I did, too," I said and swallowed the lump that was in my throat. I wanted to reach up and grab Scarlett, but more than anything I wanted this to be a moment she'd remember forever.

"I grabbed that vine and had no idea that when I crashed into you that I would be looking into the eyes of the woman I wanted to marry. That I *had* to marry," I said. "Because when I look into your eyes, I can't imagine a day without you in my life." I opened the box to reveal the emerald encrusted diamond tucked inside. "Maybe now we can tie the knot?"

Scarlett's eyes welled. "Yes, yes, yes!"

I slid the ring onto her finger. Like everything else that had happened between us, it was a perfect fit.

Epilogue

I held my camera, carefully adjusting the lenses. Though I didn't need to. His sky-blue eyes clearly came into view. *Oh, Jack.*

Emotions caught in my throat. I swallowed hard, but it didn't stop my eyes from misting. *Come on, Scarlett. You can do this.* I repositioned my camera slightly away from my face. I didn't need a flash because the sun was shining brightly in Amāre and cast its light on his beautiful strawberry-blond hair.

The wind played against the tree behind him. The aspen shook its silvery leaves as if it were announcing his arrival. Jack stood in the distance in black slacks, a black vest, dark shirt, and a golden tie. His hands were loosely in his pants pockets, his thumbs stuck out like the badass hero he was. My entire body lit up in a smile. I pressed down on the shutter release and heard my camera spin a rotation of pictures. *This is the man I'm going to marry today.*

"Isn't it bad luck or something for the groom to see the bride before the wedding?"

I shrugged. "That's what they say." I released the shutter and held my thumb over the button, ready to snap another series. "But that's the thing," I said, looking at my groom. "I'm not the bride." I peeked past the camera, but kept Jack in the frame. "I'm the wedding photographer."

His face lit up in a smile, and I pressed down on the shutter release. And in that moment, I had the perfect picture of my future husband.

****

A quartet of violins softly began to play just as a gentle rain fell. I looked up at the temperamental October sky.

Evening was upon us. Anything could happen. Just like the night I met her. *Oh, no.* I looked at Granny Hood, who was seated in the front row beside Blue and my grandmother.

Granny Hood barely shook her head. "It's okay," she mouthed.

"Rain?" I mouthed back. "What about the candles?" Pillars were staked in the ground with white candles that lined the aisle Scarlett would walk down. Granny Hood smiled and fanned away my worry. She had assured me nothing could ruin tonight's ceremony. That happily ever after would happen. So if we had to relight the candles, we would relight the candles. Yet despite the trickle of rain, the pillars glowed gently in the evening. A beacon of light for my bride-to-be. *Only in Amāre.*

I resumed my post, standing on the edge of the Dark Forest with a sentinel of trees behind me as my groomsmen. My tabby cat, Pumpkin, stood next to me as my Best Man. She rocked the black bowtie that Scarlett had draped around her neck like a strand of black pearls. *Only Pumpkin.*

The violins faded, and the cello player began. When the first chord of the wedding march struck, everyone stood. My heart beat so loudly I could hear it in my ears. I looked past the rows of white chairs and standing guests to the end, to where she would be.

Geppetto rounded the corner of chairs in a black suit with Scarlett on his arm. And in that moment, I felt the world stand still.

My God, she's beautiful.

In an ivory dress that gently draped her shoulders, tightly hugged her hourglass figure, and spilled out into a gown that sparkled with each step she took, she embodied elegance and grace. She was a beauty beyond compare. Her crimson hair flowed into spirals that were tied back with silk ribbons and crystals that shone in the moonlight that glowed upon her.

The rain suddenly stopped. I smiled with my heart as my bride approached me. *How lucky am I?*

My eyes welled. I held out my hand, and she gently placed hers in mine. The next chapter of our life was about to begin, but I already knew happily ever after wasn't just for fairytales.

The End

PUMPKIN SPICE

DEDICATION

Goldie Locks began from a clipping in the newspaper that sparked my attention: Woman Arrives Home to Find Man Sleeping in Her Bed. Isn't that how all good fairy tales begin? I took my musings to my favorite fellow writers, two blondes, who helped me with some of the inside jokes. These blondes became the basis for Rapunzel. Every Goldie has a Rapunzel in their life—I'm lucky because I have two. To DV & JW—this is for you. XOXO PS

PUMPKIN SPICE

GOLDIE LOCKS AND THE THREE BROTHERS BEAR

The Amāre Tales, 2

Pumpkin Spice

Copyright © 2016

Chapter One

"Hayden, you're going to love this."

I spun around in my chair and faced my editor, Bob, who was perched above me in the editor's box. While I coveted the bird's eye view he had of the newsroom, I didn't envy the position or stress he had overseeing the only all-news radio station in Amāre. It was hard enough competing with Internet bloggers to stay one step ahead on local and state issues, I couldn't imagine having to worry about ratings, too.

"What 'cha got?" I leaned back in my swivel chair and interlocked my fingers behind my head.

"Some gal on the East side just called the cops because she found a man asleep in her bedroom," he said.

I dropped my hands and shot forward in my chair. "And she didn't know him?"

When Bob shook his head, his black comb-over threatened to reveal the balding he refused to accept.

Balding didn't worry me, but the ever present threat of losing my six-pack and gaining a beer gut did.

"Nope," he said. "No clue. She found a complete stranger in her bed."

"No way."

"Way," Bob said. "Just heard it on the police scanner, and Delores down at Metro confirmed it."

"So what exactly happened?" I grabbed the pencil tucked behind my ear and began taking notes on my reporter notepad—a thin elongated pad that fit squarely into the palm of my hand where I placed it as I already drafted the on-air news promo that would tease the story: Woman finds stranger in bed.

"Apparently," Bob said. "She's a nurse that works the night shift. She got home this morning and found some man asleep in her bedroom."

I scratched out the headlining promo and wrote: Woman arrives home to discover … a stranger in bed. It wasn't quite hitting the mark, but if Phil read it just right on the air it could blow down the house and pull in listeners. I glanced at my empty notepad and realized Phil could read it in Swahili, if I didn't get the story I wouldn't get the listeners. "This nurse, she work at the city or state hospital?"

Bob knew what I was asking. Was this a local gal or a transplant? The Amāre city hospital hired local, but the state hospital hired whoever they could recruit.

"I'm pretty sure she's a city employee." Bob flipped through his steno pad. "Yeah, she's a city nurse."

I jotted down Amāre Medical Center, which would instantly generate on-air interest. "Did you get her name?"

When he didn't reply, I glanced up, and my editor was wildly grinning.

"Goldie," he said.

I stared at his gray-blue eyes to see if he was bluffing. Bob was part of our monthly newsroom poker game. He had been a decent player until I learned his tell—anytime he bluffed he'd occasionally blink like he had something in his eyes. His eyes weren't winking, fluttering or twitching. The old man was telling the truth.

"Her name is Goldie?" I asked just to clarify. "Like Goldie Hawn?"

He shrugged. "If she looks half that good it's your lucky day."

I rolled my eyes, grabbed my backpack and held out my hand for a set of car keys I knew Bob would toss me. "Where am I headed?" I caught the keys and address at the same time.

****

The station's news van was as outdated as the faded brown paint, white rimmed tires, and turquoise leather interior, but still it beat using my own gas and adding miles to my Mustang. I climbed into the van, programmed the East side address into my iPhone and headed toward the rich side of town. In the little mountain community of Amāre, the haves and have-nots were easy to identify. Those that had wealth lived on the East side, and those that barely had enough to survive lived on the West side. Unfortunately, I knew the dynamics all too well. My older brother lived on the East side, and my baby brother lived on the West. I lived in the middle of the two divides up on the mountain.

The neighborhood wasn't hard to find, and the red and white flashing lights from the squad car made her house easy to identify. For all the money the Eastsiders had, their homes all looked alike. Goldie's house was a cookie-cutter replica of my brother's. I pulled up to the white washed two story complete with a pristine, manicured lawn and porch swing that looked like Martha

Stewart hung it herself. Yet despite the Stepford appearance, the lights from inside the house shone against the beveled glass windows and gave it a warm yellow hue. It looked inviting. I stepped out of the news van and stared at the soft, welcoming glow. *It's no wonder the guy wanted to come inside.*

I slung my backpack over my shoulder and plugged the handheld microphone into the media player. The microphone was old school, but I found most people preferred to speak into something versus speaking into air. A microphone gave them somewhere to direct their responses.

I stepped onto the wraparound porch and immediately noticed that the ceiling was strung with mini lights. They intermittently twinkled. In the early morning light, the twinkling wasn't as brilliant as I imagined it would be if the sun wasn't competing to be seen. Even though the flickering lights were barely visible, it added a rustic charm to an ordinary East side home. I was about to knock on the front door when her voice filtered out of the open front window.

"Who is he?" Her tone peaked, but even distressed it had a certain melody to it that was captivating.

I quickly turned on the voice recorder, stuffed an earbud into my ear and aimed my handheld microphone toward the window screen. I checked the volume gauge on the media player. It was turned to the maximum setting. It allowed the faintest sound to be recorded. If the cat and fiddle kicked it up next door, I'd know. When she spoke again it was as if she was whispering in my ear.

"I've never seen him before this morning." The sincerity in her voice made me want to know more. I leaned on the window sill just out of view but closer to her.

"As I told the other officer." Her voice in my ear was hypnotic. Captivated, I pressed against the screen without any thought. "I came home from work and found a pair of shoes I didn't recognize by the front door to my house."

"Shoes?" The officer's voice wasn't as easy on the ears.

"Yes, a pair of black loafers or—I don't know, men's shoes?" Her voice sounded so familiar, but I didn't know anyone named Goldie. I inched forward on the window sill and then inched a little more. Only when I inched forward a third time, my weight shifted and I forgot that the only thing between me and this Goldie woman was a thin mesh screen. And suddenly it gave out. I crashed through the screen, fell forward, but my height and weight prevented me from falling entirely into her living room. My upper body was in her house while the other half of me was still hanging outside her window. It was like a Halloween costume gone wrong—and I was wearing both ends. If the fall didn't hurt, her ear-piercing scream did.

I tried to get myself upright, but each time I attempted it, I kept tipping back down and couldn't seem to regain my footing. I looked like the classic toy drinking bird. The only thing missing was a glass of water to dip my nose in.

I finally decided to hold myself up with one arm. Under normal circumstances, the one-arm push-up would have been quite impressive, but these weren't normal circumstances. I managed to pull the earbud out of my ear and look up as my former college roommate entered the living room. I smiled. "Hey, Burt."

"Bear, what the hell?"

"Do you know him?" Even shocked her voice was alarmingly spellbinding. I couldn't take my eyes off her.

Burt grabbed my arm and helped me to my feet. I quickly brushed off my jeans and extended my hand. "Good morning. I'm Hayden Bear with KBRU News Radio.

"Uhh…" She looked at me to Burt and back again at me. "I'm Goldie."

Her long wavy hair was as rich and golden as her name. If her golden hair didn't catch a man's interest, her eyes would. A mesmerizing shade of green with flecks of gold that seemed to shoot into a shimmering starburst of color, they were impossible not to stare into. Offset by skin that was the fairest I'd seen in all the lands I'd traveled, she was a beauty beyond compare. *Wow.*

"Goldie," I said at the young woman dressed in coral-colored hospital scrubs. Suddenly, I wanted a sponge bath.

She softly smiled, and in that smile a man could forget where he was. Or what he was supposed to be doing.

I cleared my throat. "Sorry about your screen." I pointed to the mesh mess on the hardwood floor beneath my feet. "Yeah, I'll get that fixed and returned to you. Though you probably shouldn't leave your windows open at night. Three houses across town were recently hit, and they're all owned by the Pig Construction Brothers. They said the guy who hit them was a real wolf. So open windows probably not a good idea…" As soon as I said it I wished I hadn't.

"Oh, we're going there?" Her green eyes flashed with anger, and the fairest face in all the land ignited with fury. "It wasn't the front *window* that was the problem, Mr. Bear. It was an unreliable lock that allowed a total stranger access to my house *and* my bed."

I fumbled with my media player and held out my microphone that had taken a hit when I came tumbling into her house. The mic was smashed, and the handle had dented. It looked like I was offering her a limp flower. "Would you mind repeating that?"

Her full, rose-tinted lips curved into a smile, and when she began to laugh it wasn't loud and obnoxious, nor was it high and squeaky. Hers was the perfect pitch. "You've got to be the worst or the best newsman in the industry. I'm just not sure which."

I felt my cheeks tinge with heat and tried to shrug it off. "I'm neither. Just desperate to get a story on the air before the bloggers beat me to it. And *this* is a good story."

Goldie and Burt stared at me. Only Goldie was still smiling, and I would do anything to keep that smile on her face.

"Right, well, I was hoping to get an interview about the recent events," I said.

"And you couldn't what? Knock on the door?" The tone in her voice was serious, but her playful grin wasn't.

"Well the last guy didn't so…" I snorted a laugh. Suddenly the playfulness on her face disappeared. *Nope, wrong answer.* "I should have knocked," I said to her and then glanced at Burt and gritted a smile. "I was about to knock when…"

"You heard something too good to let get by?" he said.

Yes, her voice. I nodded. "Something like that."

"Well, Bear, I'm sorry, but you won't be able to interview Miss Locks," Burt said.

"Oh, come on. It was an accident, and I said I'd pay for the repairs."

"It's not that," Burt said. "There's a conflict of interest."

I had shared a dorm room with Burt during freshman and sophomore years of college. We played a lot of poker on nights we should have been studying. His only tell was his voice. When it shifted down and low, he was either holding a killer hand or he was holding crap.

"Conflict of interest?" I weighed that Burt was bluffing to see how far I'd go to get the interview.

Burt cocked his head toward the foyer in her house.

I shook my head. "Nope. Any *conflict of interest* can be shared openly. I have no secrets."

Burt placed his hands on his hips. "The man that Miss Locks found in her bedroom."

I discreetly pressed the "record" button on my media player.

"The one that smelled like alcohol and cigars?" Goldie said. "The one I found passed out in my bedroom but not before he went into each of my guest bedrooms and tried out two other beds—that man?"

Burt nodded.

"It's the million dollar question," I said.

"Who is he?" she asked.

Conflict of interest, my ass. I extended my deformed mic toward him.

Burt looked me square in the eye. "He's still sleeping it off, but we were able to identify him. It's Dylan."

"Bear? Dylan Bear?" I asked.

Burt gave a curt nod of his head.

I took a startled step back—too far back. Goldie reached for my hand. I grabbed it before I fell back through the open window.

Chapter Two

The current that coursed through my body when our hands connected was electric, heated, and downright magnetic. He slipped his hand into mine so naturally and effortlessly it was as if I found my other half. I held onto him until he regained his footing.

"Dylan Bear. Is he related to you?" I lightened my grip, but I wouldn't let go until I had an answer.

Hayden's deep brown eyes reflected his response before he did. "Yeah, he's my older brother."

I quickly released his hand. "And you had no idea that your brother had decided to let himself into *my* house and sleep off his bender in my bed?"

Hayden shook his head.

"In Dylan's defense," Burt said. "He lives one street over, and your house looks identical to his."

Hayden raised his eyebrows. "Your house does look a lot like my brother's." He scratched the back of his head. Hair the color of wheat moved back and forth in a wave of motion. Suddenly I wanted to reach up and feel it between my fingers.

I shook my head. *Goldie, get a grip. This is crazy. You don't even know him.*

"Burt, you're sure it's Dylan. My Dylan? It's not like him to do something like this." Hayden paused.

There was something about his voice. Something about the way he defended his brother. The absolute certainty he had in him that caught in my throat. *He's loyal. This is going to be hard for him to accept.*

"Burt, you know Dylan. He's a by-the-books kind of guy," he said. "If he hasn't first planned it out, it doesn't happen."

"Is your brother about six-two, lean build, and a carries a can of dip in his back jean pocket?" I said in a gentle, reassuring tone.

Hayden volleyed his head from side-to-side. "That could be said of many guys in Amāre."

Even when the guy was in complete denial, he was cute. But cute wasn't going to speed up this process and clear half of Amāre out of my house so I could get to bed. And right now all I wanted to do was go to sleep. While it was morning to them, for me, it was the end of my shift and time for some shut-eye.

I walked toward the man whose mere touch sent shivers down my spine and spun him around until he faced my open, screen-less window. I reached up and lifted down the collar of his denim shirt. His neck was thick and led to broad shoulders that were tanned, muscular and tone. *Mercy.*

I gently touched the tattoo just under the collar of his shirt. The inked claws looked like it dug into him, but it was smooth to the touch like his skin.

He shrugged his shoulders. "What are you doing?"

"Just checking," I said and put his collar back in place. "I'm sure *everyone* in Amāre also has this identical paw print on the back of their neck like your comatose brother."

"It's our coat of arms." The definition in his cheekbones became pronounced, and his eyebrows furrowed.

Uh-oh. Touchy subject.

"It's not a *paw print,*" Hayden said. "It's a bear claw. We're one of the oldest families to homestead in Amāre. The Bear family is steeped in tradition."

I tried to mask my amusement, but I couldn't help myself. "And is part of that tradition to enter a woman's home, check out *all* her beds until they find the perfect fit, and then settle in for the night?"

When Hayden was embarrassed, his cheeks flushed and his deep inset brown eyes shone brightest. He was one bear of a man all right. I just wasn't sure I wanted him and his brother in my house. I didn't even know them.

"If," Hayden shook his misshapen microphone toward me. "And I'm not confirming it's my brother, but *if*, it *is* my brother, he would not have just entered your home unannounced. It would have been purely by accident. Dylan is the oldest Bear, and he's nothing if not responsible."

As if on cue, the sleeping Bear stumbled into my living room to join us.

"Hayden, what happened?" Dylan rubbed his head and blinked his eyes to adjust to the morning light. "Where am I?"

Hayden's face drained of color. "Oh, no." He exhaled and looked at me. "Miss Locks…"

I looked at Hayden, and if my eyes could have relayed a feeling it would have been empathy. It wasn't Hayden's fault his brother showed up unannounced in my bed.

"This is my brother, Dylan Bear." Hayden turned to his brother, who was still trying to piece together the puzzle. "Dylan, this is Miss Goldie Locks. You're in *her* house. Apparently you fell asleep here last night or sometime this morning."

When the older Bear brother smiled, a dimple surfaced on either side of his mouth. "Nuh-uh."

Hayden nodded. "Afraid so, big brother."

I stepped into the conversation and held out my hand. "I'm Goldie. This is my house."

There was absolutely, positively, no current when we touched.

"I'm in your house?" Dylan looked at me for answers. His eyes were nothing like his brother's. They were a soft shade of blue that I saw when I hiked the mountain in the spring. The wildflowers in Amāre sprang forth in a tapestry of blue that covered the countryside and truly made Amāre one of the most beautiful, wonderful places to live. While his eyes were beautiful to look at, there was no danger of getting lost in them. "How'd I end up here?"

I raised my shoulders to my ears. "You'd have to tell me. I came home from work and found your shoes outside my front door, and I eventually found you in my bedroom."

"Eventually?" His dimples reappeared.

"Well, it looks like you tried *each* bed in my guest rooms before you decided you liked my bed the best."

"Wow," he said shaking his head. "I don't know what to say. It's not like me—at all. I'm really sorry."

The brothers Bear wore sincerity well, and Dylan wore it best. There was no doubt he wasn't someone that ended up in strange beds often, if ever. The guy was harmless. The fact that he was easy on the eyes didn't hurt either.

"I went out with the guys last night," he said and turned to his brother. "It was Jack's last hurrah before his honeymoon. So we went out after we closed down the winery."

I tilted my head and studied his profile. *It couldn't be.* I angled myself to get a better look, and in the right shadow his silhouette came into view. *No way.* The small nose, jutted out chin and long neck. It was the same silhouette that appeared on my favorite bottle of honey wine. "Oh. My. Gosh. You're Bear? As in Bear Trap Winery? That's you?"

Dylan raised his right palm. "Guilty as charged." He turned to Burt. "We went out after work to wish Jack good luck on his new adventure." Dylan looked at me. "After Jack harvested a bean field and the stocks on his crop paid off he hit some financial troubles. But then he worked with the SEC where he met Scarlett Hood." He rolled his eyes. "Well, that's an entirely other story. Suffice to say we took him out last night, and I..." Dylan shook his head. His hair wasn't nearly as textured or blond as his brother's. But the guy could sport a buzz cut better than most. "Anyway, I must have had one too many maple shots, and ... uh..."

"Ah, the savory sap," I said. "I know its effects all too well." The oldest Bear and purveyor of my favorite honey pot wine barely acknowledged my attempt to connect with him. Hayden, on the other hand, who had been oddly quiet, remerged and found a way to weave his microphone between me and his brother.

"Listen, my editor just texted and I was wondering if we could go live with this interview." He looked at me and then his brother and finally to Burt. "Unless of course, you're going to file charges?"

"That's entirely up to Miss Locks," Burt said.

I was still gawking at Dylan's profile when I realized that was my cue. "Oh, charges?" I rolled my shoulders forward and talked with my hands. "It's not like he did anything other than make a mess of the hospital corners on my perfectly made beds, but," I shook my head, "no, I'm not going to file charges. It was clearly a mistaken identity of homes."

Relief washed over Dylan's face, and excitement sparked in Hayden's eyes. "So? What do you think? Would you two be willing to go live on the radio?"

This guy was annoyingly persistent and charming at the same time. I wasn't sure if it was a turn-on or turn-off. I just knew that I wouldn't get to any of my beds and much needed sleep if he didn't get this story on the air.

"What the heck," I said. "You game?" I flashed a smile at Dylan.

"Why not? It's not every day I wind up in a beautiful woman's house—let alone her bed."

I felt my body spike with heat. *Wowza. Is Mr. Honey Pot flirting with me?*

"Okay, all right, let's get this thing started," Hayden's tone was clipped. He quickly texted something to his editor and pressed the red button on his media player. "This will relay the interview to the radio station. There's a five second delay in case you accidentally curse or say something you shouldn't." He shot both me and Dylan a warning with his eyes. "So let's have fun, but nothing that has to be delayed on the air, okay?"

We both nodded.

Hayden held up his hand and counted down to five with his fingers. When his fist closed, the red light on his media player rapidly blinked.

"Good morning, Amāre, I'm here live with local resident and nurse, Miss Goldie Locks who returned home this morning to…" Hayden smiled in my direction. "Well, Goldie, why don't you tell our listeners what happened?"

He tilted the deformed mic toward me, and even though I knew we were on the radio, it felt like I was only talking to him. And talking to Hayden already seemed as natural to me as working an emergency room. It just fit. I looked into his brown eyes and smiled.

"Well, Hayden, when I walked into my house this morning, I immediately knew something was wrong. But oddly," I turned to Dylan. "I wasn't scared." I then glanced back to Hayden and coyly raised my eyebrow. "But I did think, '*Who's been sleeping in my bed?*'"

Hayden pumped his fist in the air, and I couldn't help but giggle. He cocked his head toward his brother. "And for you, sir, what was it like to wake up in someone else's house?"

"Regretful that I caused any distress to Miss Locks," Dylan said and coyly lowered his head. "I had a friend drive me home after I went to a work celebration. I must have mistaken her house for mine." He glanced at me, his blue eyes pensive. "Goldie, please accept my apologies. Perhaps I can even make it up to you?"

Hayden kept the microphone between us, and the red light on his recorder blinked as fast as my heart.

I tilted my head and let my hair fall down my shoulder. I twisted a lock with my finger. "Make it up to me?" I said playfully for whoever was listening.

"I'd like to take you out to dinner," Dylan said in a honeyed voice. "And I promise I won't end up in your bed unless you invite me."

Suddenly, the microphone fell, and the airwaves went silent.

Chapter Three

In the merry village of Amāre, love wasn't just the town's namesake. It seemed a way of life. So yesterday when my brother asked Goldie out to dinner, I wasn't thrilled, but I also wasn't going to be the reason their date didn't happen. *I mean what's the harm in one date? It's not like he's taking her somewhere romantic.* That wasn't in Dylan's wheelhouse.

My iPhone buzzed with an incoming text. **Hey, bro, thinkin of taking Goldie 2 The Magic Oven. U still have an in w/the owner?**

The Magic Oven? Dylan's never taken a woman to The Magic Oven. *What the hell? That's my…* I tapped my finger to my chest. *My first date place.* I looked around the newsroom, but no one seemed to notice my internal rant. I scratched the back of my head. *The Magic Oven, huh? Oh, yeah, I've got an in with the owner, but I'm not so sure I'm going to call Hansel and ask him or his sister Gretel to reserve my favorite table or cook up a special batch of Raclette.* I drew a deep breath. When I exhaled, I could practically taste their signature dish on my tongue.

Just the thought of roasted, melted cheese made my mouth water. There was *nothing* more romantic than introducing a woman to an evening of Raclette with our own private fireplace and a wheel of cheese. No matter who I took to The Magic Oven the reaction was always the same—the ambiance and food evoked an instant attraction. There hadn't been a woman yet who wasn't surprised and delighted when the cheese wheel was placed on the fire. We'd watch it cook until it reached the perfect softness, and then Hansel or Gretel would remove the fire-roasted cheese that would melt onto the top of freshly baked baguettes. It was a meal that made happily ever after a reality. I could only imagine Goldie sitting tableside by the fire. She would be the only woman whose golden hair and starlit eyes would generate more heat than the open flame. And the taste of her rose-tinted lips would be grander than the meal itself.

I slammed my hand down on my desk. Bob didn't even move from his perch or look down at me. Editors were used to temperamental reporters.

"Magic Oven," I mumbled under my breath. "Yeah, whatever." I scrolled through my contacts and texted Dylan the link to Hansel's private line. I hit "send" and heard the familiar "ding" indicating that my text had been sent. *Great. Go knock yourself out, big brother. You're on a roll. End up in beauty's bed and now dinner. Whatever.*

I shook my head and glanced up at Bob. "You wanna catch a movie?" I skimmed my laptop for the online movie listings. "Oh, yeah. The Brothers Grimm have a new flick that starts tonight. It's called *The Two Brothers*. Huh." I zoomed in on the screen to read the synopsis. "*The Two Brothers* is about a rich, evil brother and a poor, good brother." I leaned back in my chair. "Well, I'm sure the latter brother ends up victorious. He's got to, right?" I glanced up at Bob, who was shaking his head.

"Nah," Bob said. "Doesn't sound like one I'd want to see. They probably fight over something stupid and end up penniless. Nope, I like the Grimm Brothers' lighter films like *Looking For A Bride*, or *The True Bride*, great movies where love prevails over evil. Love stories are always more satisfying."

I waved him away.

"Why don't you ask that woman you met while you were covering that gala?"

"What woman? Which gala?" There were so many events I was sent to cover for the radio station that they all started to blur.

"You know that Midnight gala—you met Cinders-something and her two sisters."

"Her name is Cinder Ella, and they're her stepsisters," I clarified.

Bob shrugged. "What's the difference? I thought you liked one of them."

"I liked Cinder, but she met a guy that night." I leaned back in my chair. "She was in such a rush to get home by curfew that she lost her shoe. He found it, tracked her down." I held up my index finger. "But not in a creepy way. He scoured the town with that stiletto until he found its rightful owner. And the rest is how we hope stories like that end." I opened my hands like I was releasing a handful of pixie dust. "Happy. Cinder's happy. And apparently he turned out to be a real prince of a guy, so I can't fault her for that. When you find the one, you find the one."

I rocked back and forth in my chair until the suspension creaked like a rusty tin man. It was an annoying sound, but I'd do anything to get Goldie off my mind. "You know one of Cinder's stepsisters wasn't so bad."

"Ask her to the movies," Bob said.

I shook my head. "Nah. There's no interaction in a movie. You go to a movie with someone you don't care if you interact with."

Bob scoffed. "Nice to know that's why you invited me."

"Ah, get over it. It's a movie." I rapped my hands against my desk. "But dinner." I snapped. "That's when you get to know someone."

"So take her to dinner."

Bob was my editor, poker buddy, counselor, and usually stand-in movie date. He wore many hats and wore them all well.

"Why not? I could do dinner with … uh…" I thought back to the gala event. Cinder's sister wasn't nearly as striking, but her name wasn't half-bad. *What was it?* I tapped my fingers on the keyboard to my laptop and did a quick internet search of Cinder's recent engagement. Her two stepsisters stood beside her in the photo and looked about as happy as Cinder's stepmother. I skimmed the photo cutline that listed the names. "Anastasia! That's it. Her name's Anastasia."

"Yeah, probably helpful to know the woman's name before you ask her out," Bob said with his head down and a red ballpoint pen in his hand.

"That isn't my copy you're editing, is it?"

He ignored me.

"You know this is radio. As long as the anchors can read it, it doesn't matter if I misspelled a word or forgot a comma or period."

He shook his head. "Keep telling yourself that, Hayden. Commas create a necessary pause and break for the anchor. It allows the story to flow forward the way it was intended to be read. Not like the way you write."

"What's wrong with the way I write?"

"If it weren't for my commas and copy editing the anchor would never get a chance to come up for air. You're the king of long, run-on sentences."

"Whatever. It's not like I talk in long, run-on, rambling sentences that lead nowhere without a point. I'm usually pretty succinct, and besides, the audience *loved* yesterday's feature I did on Goldie." When I came up for air, Bob was shaking his head.

"Actually, that was some solid reporting. You handled that interview well. And on the fly no less."

I raised my eyebrows. "I'm nothing if not quick on my feet."

"Well it didn't hurt that Miss Locks was a natural on the air," Bob said.

"Yeah, she was something."

"Why don't you ask her out?" Bob said.

"My brother already beat me to it." The truth flew out of my mouth, and I wasn't on the air where I could hit the delay switch. *Damn.*

"Oh," Bob slowly nodded. "So that's what's got you in such a foul mood, Grumpy."

I held up my index finger. "I'm not Grumpy or Sleepy or any of those reckless wonders that own that bar."

When Bob laughed his years of smoking a pipe revealed itself in his wheeze. I knew it wasn't a healthy sound, but it nonetheless made me grin.

"The best way to get over a woman is to take another woman out to dinner," Bob said.

"I don't think that's how the expression goes."

Bob smiled. "Go have fun. Be young. Court someone new."

I stared at the photo of Anastasia on the computer screen. From a distance, she looked dateable. *What the hell.* I picked up the phone on my desk and called down to the photo department who had snapped and posted the picture to our online photo gallery. The call was picked up before it had a chance to ring.

"Bear, whose number you need now?"

A sideways smile slid on my face. "Listen, Red, how do you know I need someone's number? And I thought you were off on your honeymoon."

Her laughter was throaty and sexy as hell. "First, it's Scarlett, not Red. Second, I leave for my honeymoon straight after work, so don't get me fired before then. And third, you *only* call down to the photo department when you spot some princess you claim you've got to call for some story when, really, we both know you're just fishing for a date."

Scarlett was someone I had tried to take out, but she literally already knew my number. Besides, anytime I got close to her she either hid behind her wavy, red hair or tried to disappear behind that ridiculous gray hoodie she always wore. Besides *that*, now she was taken.

"Don't hate the player," I said.

She laughed again. "Whose number am I risking my job for now, Bear?"

"Anastasia. She's one of Cinder Ella's stepsisters. I met her at the midnight ball."

"Oh, well, isn't this interesting," Scarlett said.

I pressed my ear into the receiver. "What?"

"A local baker just called for the exact same number, hmmm," she said.

"A baker?" I rolled my eyes. "I'm not worried about some baker. Give up the digits, Scarlett, and no one gets hurt."

Again, her laughter. "Got a pen?"

"Don't I always?" I jotted down the series of seven numbers that began and ended with three. "Thanks, Red."

The call had barely disconnected when I used the company phone to dial out. Residents of Amāre were friendly folk, but having the local radio station pop up on caller ID practically guaranteed to get someone to pick up the phone.

"Hello? This is Anastasia."

Her voice wasn't as lyrical as Goldie's or as sexy as Scarlett's, but it wasn't bad. "Anastasia, hello. It's Hayden Bear from KBRU Radio. I met you at the midnight ball…" I paused so she could make the connection.

"Of course, you're one of the Bear brothers, right?"

I grinned. "Yup. I'm the middle Bear."

"How are you?" Her voice was warming to me. I stared at her picture on my laptop screen. *This could be fun.*

"Well, I'm good. I was wondering if you'd like to go out to dinner?"

"Tonight?" There was a shift in the conversation.

"If tonight's too soon, we could…" *Damn, maybe this other guy beat me to it.*

"No, no it's not that. I was just expecting this baker … you know, tonight would be wonderful."

I slowly nodded. A baker? Who the heck is this guy? "That'd be fantastic," I said. *Fake it 'til you make it.* "I know it's kind of last minute, but…." *I've got to do something to get Goldie out of my head.*

"No, tonight's perfect. I could use a night out," she said. "How about The Magic Oven? I hear it's amazing."

My shoulders dropped, and so did my spirits. "Yeah, it's a great little restaurant—I even know the owners."

"Perfect!" Her voice shifted into high gear and giddy.

"The Magic Oven it is. I'll pick you up at seven." I hung up the phone and stared at the receiver. *What the hell did I just get myself into?*

Chapter Four

Nestled on a little bluff on the mountainside of Amāre, a ginger-colored cottage with frosted window panes and smoke filtering from the chimney welcomed travelers from far and wide. The door to The Magic Oven opened, and a beautiful, young woman emerged. She welcomed Dylan and me into her home that doubled as a restaurant.

"I'm Gretel, and I promise delicious food awaits you," she said with a smile.

I gushed. "This is so much fun," I said toward Dylan, who seemed ill at ease. "Are you okay?"

He curtly nodded and followed Gretel as she led us to a fireside table. Dylan held out my chair. I draped my silk wrap along the high back and tucked my yellow checkered dress beneath me. Dylan pushed my chair into the table, only a little too far. I held up a finger.

"Kinda want to breathe this evening," I said laughing. "Though this table could come in handy if we ever need to do the Heimlich maneuver."

Dylan's face remained unchanged.

"Didn't like my hospital humor?" *Bummer. My corny jokes usually work when I admit a nervous patient into the ER.*

Dylan shook his head. "I'm sorry. I'm really new to this."

"Huh." I gently pushed my chair back from the table. "The other day you seemed like asking me out was as natural as…" I shrugged. "I don't know a bear chasing honey—or in your case making honey pot wine."

Finally Dylan laughed, and I relaxed. "See, it's that easy," I said. "We're just two *complete* strangers having dinner at the most romantic place in all of Amāre. No pressure."

His blue eyes softened like rain. "I can see why Hayden wanted to interview you."

"Hayden? I don't know if he *wanted* to interview me as much as he *had* to interview me." I slightly chuckled. "When a woman calls nine-one-one because she's found a man sleeping in her bed it doesn't take much thought that it'd be a good story—or at least an interesting one. No," I shook my head and felt my hair bounce on my shoulders, "I think your brother was just doing his job when he ended up at my little house."

Dylan leaned toward the table. "That may be true, but I know my brother and the way he looked at you." Dylan reached across the table for my hand. "Hayden was smitten with you. *He* should be sitting here with you, not me."

His hand was clammy, and I knew from taking enough pulses that when the body was in any type of crisis, adrenaline caused a decrease in the blood flow to areas like the hands. Clammy hands meant anxiety. *He's nervous.* Albeit a date with Hayden had crossed my mind, I was out with the eldest Bear. I was going to make the best of a very awkward situation.

I gently squeezed his hand to pump blood back into them. "But I didn't come home to find Hayden sleeping in my bed – or making a mess *of* my other two beds."

Dylan leaned his head back and laughed. And suddenly his hands warmed beneath my touch.

****

My brother's laughter rose above the fireplace that separated our tables. I slipped Gretel a twenty to keep him and Goldie's date out of my eyeshot. I didn't think I'd have to worry about hearing them. *Great. Just freakin' wonderful.*

"So obviously you've eaten here before," Anastasia said, bobbing her head. Long, brunette-colored, sausage-like curls hung around her plump face.

No wonder the baker has the hots for her. "I have been here, and the food is delicious," I said.

Anastasia smiled. She was dressed in pink from head to toe. A splash of purple on her slipper-footed feet was the only thing to break up the dose of Pepto-Bismol that came at me when she placed her arms on the table. "So what's yummy?"

Goldie? I gritted my teeth to squelch the laughter that threatened to erupt from the empty pit of my stomach. I was probably the only guy that laughed at his own jokes. "The Magic Oven is known for its Raclette. I already took the liberty of ordering it for us."

"What?" Her voice could have broken glass. "You *ordered* my meal? What century do you think we live in?"

"The twenty-first?" *Is this a trick question?*

She crossed her thick arms over her ample chest. "I'll have you know, Mr. Bear, that my mother raised me to be an independent woman. I make my own choices. It is only by making my own choices that I will live the life I want and deserve."

I nodded like an obedient dog. "Okay, I'm terribly sorry. I can get Hansel to prepare whatever you'd like."

Her steely eyes steadied me. She unlocked her arms and fanned her hand toward me. "Oh, I'm just giving you a hard time." She fluttered her thick eyelashes. "I like to see what a man's made of."

Please don't put me in the oven and eat me. I held my breath.

"I'm sure this Raclette is fine, but if you wouldn't mind getting Hansel to drum up some chicken fingers and home fries that'd be swell."

I quickly exited the table and silently prayed a magical nymph would fly down and carry me away. I was so rattled that I turned right at the fireplace when I should have headed straight toward the kitchen. But damn if my date's sudden smack-down didn't get me turned all around. Suddenly I came face-to-face with Goldie.

"Look who showed up for some dinner," she said playfully.

Dylan spun in his chair, and his face was ashen.

"Brother, are you all right?" I was at his side in a minute.

He shook his head. "Ah, I'm just." He shrugged. "You know me. I'm all work and no play."

I gave him a hearty pat on the back. "That's why I was so proud of you when you asked Miss Locks out to dinner." Color began to filter back into my brother's cheeks. "Besides the fact that you probably *owed* her some form of apology for ending up in her bed unannounced." I winked at Goldie. "I think it's great you're out on a weeknight and not home mastering some new honey pot wine."

"Now, let's not go crazy," Goldie said with a return wink. "We want Dylan to master some new version of honey pot wonderfulness. His wine is the best thing to touch my lips in a long time."

I bit my lip to stop the instant retort that wanted to fly from my mouth.

"So who are you with?" Goldie looked around the restaurant.

Now I felt my face drain of all life. I lowered my voice along with my head. "I'm here with Anastasia."

"Oh, isn't she Cinder Ella's half-sister?" Goldie asked.

I clapped my hands together loudly and startled us both. "Step. They're stepsisters." I eyed Goldie. "I don't think there's *any* relation between them." I slowly shook my head and waved my hands like an umpire calling a play. "Like none. No relation whatsoever."

Goldie's laughter was like a song whose melody I had always searched for. She awakened my soul, and I'd sit at her feet if it meant I could be in her company. "Would you like to join us?" she asked.

I clasped my hands tightly together to prevent myself from cupping her porcelain face and kissing her full rose-tinted lips. "No, but thank you."

Dylan elbowed me. "You should join us. It'd be fun."

I released my hands and pointed toward the kitchen. "Nothing will be fun unless I get to the kitchen and back to my table before the Raclette does." I wiped my face with my hand, but it didn't erase how awful I felt. This night was just not shaping up the way I had hoped.

"Hayden?" My brother's voice was filled with concern.

"Oh, it's nothing a little chicken fingers won't fix," I said with a weak attempt at a smile.

"Are you okay?" When Goldie stood, I caught my breath. Her yellow dress was outlined in a layer of sheer lace that bordered and hugged every curve of her delicious body. The neckline to her dress dipped just enough to see a hint of cleavage. *Is that even legal?*

"Wow. You look amazing," I said the words falling out of my mouth.

When she twirled, her skirt kicked up to reveal layers of more lace. "Ah, thank you, brother Bear. I thought it was time to get out of my scrubs and into something pretty."

I couldn't speak. Her golden locks were pulled back by a yellow bow that matched her dress. *Damn.* I eyed her Mary Jane high heels, white stockings, and ruffled, lacey anklets that hugged her skinny legs. *I wonder whose bed she'll be sleeping in tonight?* Her outfit was just on the polite side of naughty.

"Pretty is an understatement." I cleared my throat. "Well, I'd better get back to my table."

"Don't forget the kitchen," Goldie said.

My mind went blank.

"You said you needed to go to the kitchen?" Dylan said.

I snapped. "Right. I've got to change her order."

I tried to regain my composure, but unlike the startled, hurried, and unwanted feeling that Anastasia provoked, Goldie made everyone she encountered feel welcomed. I could see it on my brother's face, and I felt it in every pore of my being. Goldie was the real deal. I wanted to ditch my date and be a third wheel on theirs. Instead, I headed toward the kitchen to salvage the rest of my night.

****

I watched Hayden leave. In a pair of dark jeans that snuggled his ass, navy dress shirt with sleeves rolled up, and a black vest, he wore western well. I turned to Dylan, who was watching me watch his brother. I quickly looked down at my dinner plate.

"This looks delicious," I said picking at the melted cheese and wrapping a strand around the tines of my fork.

"Hayden's a good guy," he said.

For a moment, I closed my eyes and tried to remember everything my first nursing teacher ever taught me about patient-care when I was in school. Even though Dylan wasn't a patient, the rules applied. And sometimes breaking the rules in order to serve the greater good was needed. So when a patient knew that their diagnosis wasn't favorable, what they needed to hear wasn't what they already knew. Sometimes what they needed most was to feel something they rarely felt. With my eyes closed, I heard the faint sound of music. I opened my eyes and looked into his soft baby blues and smiled.

"Would you care to dance?"

His face answered with the response that everyone at some point in their life needed to have—hope.

The dance floor was empty. Dylan looked at me. "Are you sure we should dance?"

I twirled and let my dress kick up. "And ruin showing this little number off?" I rolled my shoulders and inched my finger toward him as I made my way toward the center of the floor. "Come on, Brother Bear. Dance with me."

In a pair of khakis and red pullover, he looked like he belonged in a department store stocking shelves. I grabbed his hand and pulled him into me. He was at least six inches taller than I was, and that difference placed me directly in the center of his chest. He smelled like honey. I looked up at him and grinned.

"You smell good enough to eat." His cheeks burned bright red. "I mean it," I said. "I love your wine, and you smell just like your vintage honey flavor."

"Occupational hazard," he said and raised an eyebrow. "Though now it seems to be a benefit." He quickly pulled me into him and then released me just as swiftly as the tempo of the music increased.

Hell yeah! I smiled brightly as my dress flew out and in, and my spirits soared as the eldest Bear seemed to find his footing.

"I love the colorful clothes you wear. From your orange scrubs to your yellow dresses," he said in my ear.

I looked up at him and smiled. "Not too much?"

He shook his head. "No, bright colors they really become you." He paused for a moment. "It's your thing."

His compliment was so awkward, it was oddly charming. I placed my hand on his chest. "Ahh, Dylan. Thank you."

As I stood in his arms, I knew that the eldest Bear had ended up in my bed for a reason. Maybe it was to regain his footing on the dance floor. Or in dating. Who knows? All I knew was that he had a sparkle in his eyes that I wasn't about to diminish.

The music began to fade, and his eyes softened. "It's been a while since I've been on a date," he said.

"I never would have known." I leaned up and gently kissed his cheek. There was no passion, no energy, or promise. There wasn't anything but friendship exchanged in that kiss, but from the look in Dylan's eyes it was enough. "I've had a wonderful evening," I said.

Dylan squeezed my hand. "Let's go eat and get drunk on my honey-pot wine!"

I raised my shoulders to my ears. "I thought you'd never ask."

****

The chicken fingers and home fries made it to our table just as I heard Goldie's voice between the fire place that separated our tables.

"I'm starved," she said sounding breathless. "Oh, my gosh! This is amazing."

Inwardly I smiled. *Her first taste of Raclette.*

"I didn't think anything could taste so good," Goldie said.

I looked at my plate of chicken fingers and sighed. *Maybe next time.*

"What *is* she eating?" Anastasia's voice pierced the blessed silence that had been between us since our chicken-filled meal had been delivered.

"She's probably having the Raclette," I said without trying to hide the cynicism.

"Hmmm." Anastasia crossed her legs, and her feet clad in purple ballet slippers suddenly seemed enormous.

"Wow. What size shoe do you wear?" I knew as soon as the question popped out of my mouth that it was incredibly rude, but we had long passed pleasantries and good manners when she placed her fork onto my plate after she polished off her meal and began eating mine.

Something that resembled laughter rasped from her throat. "I'm a size thirteen. Momma has to have special shoes made just for me."

"No doubt." *It's no wonder her foot didn't fit into the stiletto the prince scoured the city with. I'm surprised she didn't break the shoe before Cinder Ella was able to slip it back on.*

"This is the best meal I have ever had," Goldie's voice softly filtered through the wood smoke and into my ear like a whisper. Melancholy tugged at my heart. *I should have been the one introducing her to Raclette.*

"I've got to know what she's having." Anastasia hefted herself from the table.

"Where are you going?" Panic gripped my voice.

"Well, duh, to try a taste. Didn't you say your brother was on the other side of the fireplace?"

"I did, but that's only because you asked why I had taken so long to get back to the table." I sounded as pathetic as I felt. *I sure hope the baker is up to the task of dating the stepsister from hell.* I know I wasn't man enough.

"Well, then, let's go. Let's go try a bite." She reached for my hand, and I vehemently shook my head.

"No." The tone in my voice was slightly raised. But it didn't give Anastasia any pause. She pushed away from the table, and her dress kicked up. But instead of seeing shimmering yellow satin or lace like I had on Goldie, I was submerged in a sea of pink.

I remained seated with my arms crossed over my empty stomach. My date had gobbled down most of my meal. But I was not going to rescue her from herself. *Nope. She's on her own.*

She briskly walked away, and I listened intently. But there was nothing to hear. I leaned over our table and looked through the fireplace, but the flame was too high and too bright. All I could see was my date's big, giant purple feet. *Hell, three blind mice could spot those boats.*

I got up from the table and inched around the corner of the brick fireplace. My date was sitting in Goldie's chair eating her food. *What the hell? Where's Goldie? Did she eat her, too?*

I glanced, but I didn't see Dylan or Goldie in either direction. *Crappity, crap, crap.* If I don't stop her, she's going to eat the entire wheel of smoked cheese. When I suddenly appeared in front of the table, Anastasia didn't even bother to look up. She continued to dip pieces of Goldie's perfectly torn apart baguette into the pot of Raclette. Hansel had served it to them old-school fondue-style. Instead of shavings of melted cheese, they had a pot of gooey goodness to dip into. It was romantic as hell, and Anastasia was eating what was left of my brother's first date in a very long time. *Hells to the no.*

"Stop eating and get up from the table," I said in an authoritative voice that made Anastasia actually take note.

"Just one more bite," she said with her plump cheeks overloaded with bread and cheese.

"No." I held out my hand.

She slapped it away.

I shook my head and gritted my teeth. "Listen let's not make more of a scene than we already have."

"This is delicious," she said and dipped the last piece of Goldie's baguette into the fondue.

I hit my breaking point. I gently reached for her forearm, but I'd tackled linesman with smaller arms than this woman. "It's time to go."

Anastasia pushed away from the table, but her ginormous feet got trapped in the tablecloth. I watched in slow motion as she fell toward me. I braced for impact, but my date and her feet came crashing down on me. It wasn't just her curled hair that looked like sausage links; she smelled like them, too. I held my breath, but it did nothing to mask the very strong and unappetizing scent of garlic, pepper, and onion that hit me and hit me hard. It was like getting slammed upside the head by an Italian meat cart.

When we finally untangled ourselves, I brushed myself off and glanced at the table. The place settings were strewn, and cheese dripped off the sides of the fondue pot. Otherwise nothing needed to be replaced other than Goldie's entire meal.

"Oh, don't worry about the mess. I'll call my stepsister, Cinder, and have her clean it up. She's good that way," Anastasia said.

I closed my eyes and wished I could click the heels of my boots together three times and be home or anywhere other than where I was. When I opened my eyes, Gretel was within reach. I flagged her over. She immediately stood before me.

"Could you please bring a new batch of Raclette and bill me?" I looked at the crumbs left on Goldie's plate. "And fresh bread? I know it's getting late, but do you think Hansel could bake a new batch of baguettes?"

Gretel smiled in my direction, and it was a welcomed sight. "Anything for our favorite brother Bear."

"Thank you."

I turned to Anastasia and was about to end what never should have started when Goldie walked up behind her.

"Oh, no," she said when she saw the disheveled table. "Someone's been eating off my plate." She walked past me and Anastasia and gasped. "And it's all gone."

Goldie turned, not to me, but to my brother. "What happened?"

Dylan looked like a deer caught in the headlights.

"It's my fault!" I blurted out. "I came to introduce you to my date, saw your plate of food, and boy, did it look yummy." I patted my stomach for good measure. "So," I shrugged with wide, opened eyes, "I just helped myself."

When Goldie laughed it wasn't deep and throaty like Scarlett, nor was it high-pitched and annoying like Anastasia. When Goldie laughed it was just the right blend of sensuality and femininity that made a man feel like he was the funniest person in the room. When in reality, I was the biggest joke.

"You ate her entire meal?" Dylan looked horrified. "We just left to get a drink from the bar. In that time, you ate her *entire* meal?"

My stomach growled and didn't help sell my story. "Yup, that's right." I waved my hand over the table like a magician. "Ate the whole thing."

Goldie continued to laugh. "Oh, Hayden."

"But replacements are coming. I've already ordered a new pot of Raclette and baguettes," I said. "And it's on me." I tapped my chest. "The entire meal. On me."

Goldie knelt down beside me, tucked her beautiful dress beneath her knees and gently stroked my arm. "You didn't have to do that."

Her touch sent shocks throughout my body and awakened every dormant cell. "It's the *least* I could do." I stared into her green eyes with flecks of gold, and for a moment I felt like we were all alone. And for more than a moment, I wished we were.

"Are we going to order dessert?" Anastasia's voice brought me back to the grim reality that some women were just better suited for movie dates.

Chapter Five

I barely slowed my Mustang in front of her house. "Aren't you going to walk me to the door?"

I turned my head to Anastasia and let the V8 in my classic '68 idle loudly. I cupped my hand around my ear. "What?"

"I thought you could come in for a nightcap."

I may have stepped on the gas pedal to drown out her voice. "Thanks for a great night!" My voice was as chipper as I could muster as I reached across a sea of pink chiffon for the passenger's side door handle. I opened it. She politely smiled before exiting my car. I tried to wave away the smell of Italian sausage she left behind, but I knew it'd be a while before that bouquet left my ride.

Still, I waited until my date was inside her mother's house and the front porch lights were turned off before I dropped the clutch and left skid marks in my wake. My Mustang tore up the back roads of Amāre in a blaze of fire.

Never again. I don't care if I end up alone.

It was an empty threat, and I knew it. I drove toward the moon that hung low in the evening sky. The faster I drove the closer it came to me. I smiled.

"I'm closing in on you, and then we'll find out if you're really made of cheese." I patted my stomach. "I still haven't eaten. And you know how much I love a good wheel of cheese."

So the chase was on. I honed my sights on the man in the moon, or whoever sat brightly in the night sky and gave lovers a reason to believe in fairy tales and happily ever after. I was going to get to that moon or to the end of Amāre's town limits, I just wasn't sure which would happen first. My cell phone glowed with an incoming text. I reluctantly pulled to the side of the road.

Hayden, think ur date left behind her silk wrap & Dylan left w/o his Raclette. We're still open— Hansel

I exhaled and rapped my thumbs against my cell. *Silk wrap?* I volleyed my head from side-to-side. *I don't remember a silk wrap.* I glanced up at the sky that was shifting colors. "You lucked out, buddy. I'll get you next time." I texted Hansel.

Ur a doll. On my way. Give me 5.

As soon as Gretel handed me the silk wrap that was the color of homespun butter and lingered with the scent of gardenia petals and a hint of apricot nectar I knew who it belonged to. It practically slipped through my fingers, but I let that happen once before and I wasn't about to let it happen again. I held onto it tightly. I looked up at Gretel.

"Do you think it's too late?" I said. "You know, to return it?"

Her brown eyes warmed back at me softly, and she smiled. "Hayden, it's never too late."

I nodded. "Okay, then." I turned to leave when she tapped me on my shoulder. I pivoted on the heel of my boot.

"Your Raclette?" She handed me a take-out box. Its weight alone made my stomach grumble.

"Right." I grinned. "Thanks for making another order. I can't believe Dylan didn't stay to finish this."

"He seemed in a hurry to leave."

Of course. All the air left my lungs. "He was on a date with Goldie. He probably had other plans."

Gretel shook her head. "No, I don't think that's what it was about. I just think the night had come to a natural conclusion."

"Huh." I held onto the box of cheese and the silk wrap—both felt warm to the touch.

Gretel walked to the door and held it open. "So I imagine she's still hungry."

I shook my head. "What?"

"When you bring Goldie her wrap, make sure you share the Raclette. I don't think she was able to truly enjoy our signature dish."

I gently bowed my head toward the hostess I absolutely adored and who knew me so well. "*That* is a promise."

****

My Mustang seemed to know the way to her home. Unlike the dark and desolate back roads, the main streets were gently lit by lamps that hung on each corner, welcoming travelers from far and wide to the town of Amāre. The night sky continued to shift in color and mood. The evening shade of sapphire had darkened as midnight seemed ready to make a grand entrance. Nothing was different, yet possibility seemed to linger in the air. I looked at the silk wrap on my passenger seat and the to-go box of Raclette, which were both safely strapped in by a seat belt. When it came to cheese and specifically Raclette, one could never be too sure.

I glanced in my rearview mirror. The moon seemed to be following me. I raised my eyebrows and wagged my finger. "Uh-huh. You know I've got my own cheese, don't you?" I shook my head. "Nope. Not sharing. Not with *you* anyway."

The moon didn't seem to heed my warning. It cast its mellow glow behind me while I made my way into her subdivision. Her house was one block away from Dylan's, but when I pulled up beside the front, it no longer reminded me of my brother's home. My stomach filled with butterflies. *Come on, Hayden, get a grip, man.*

I wiped my hands on my jeans, unbuckled the box of food and gently grabbed her silk wrap. I hit the door handle with my elbow and carefully pushed my way out of the car. The front walk to her house was lit by the same twinkling lights that I had noticed were strung on the ceiling of her wraparound porch. They intermittently twinkled, and I felt like I had stepped into a dream. As I walked forward, the lights flickered, keeping rhythm with my heart that beat in short little spurts the closer I got to her door.

The last time I entered her home, I fell through the window. *Let's not do that again.* I took a deep breath and rapped my knuckles on the monolithic oak door in front of me. The massive barrier seemed to block out not only light but time and space itself, and I wondered what disaster on the other side of it might be held back only by the pair of quivering, rusted steel hinges straining under its weight.

Shockingly my knock elicited no response.

I tapped my boot on the slates of her wooden porch. I shifted the to-go box to my side, slung her wrap around my neck like a scarf and decided to give her door a real good Bear-sized thump. I cocked back my arm, extended my fist all the way, lifted my front shoulder, and stepped back. I determined the exact spot on the door that I was going to rap and focused my sights on it. Just as I quickly swung forward with all my body weight from my back foot to my front foot to give that oak door a solid, it suddenly swung open. My fist came forward and struck, not the oak door as I had intended, but jabbed Goldie right square in the jaw.

Her head snapped back and then forward. Dazed, she started to wobble toward me. "Did you just punch me?"

I barely nodded. *Oh, my God.* My body flushed with shock, then horror, and then a shot of adrenaline. "Are you okay?" I rushed toward her and held out my arms as she swayed from sided-to-side holding her chin. The to-go box dropped from beneath me with a loud thud as its contents spilled all over her porch.

"Is that cheese?" She looked at the warm Raclette that oozed out of the box in velvety, creamy ribbons.

Again I nodded. "Yup," I said looking at my second lost supper of the evening. "But that doesn't even matter. I don't care. How's your mouth?"

She glanced up at me. Her tongue began to play with her lip that was suddenly twice its normal size and as purple as the night sky had turned.

I covered my mouth with my hand. *Oh no!*

"Hay-wen, you all-white?"

I shook my head. "Yeah, I'm good."

She giggled. "You don't seem all-white."

"Let's get you inside and get some ice." I cocked my head toward the front door.

Goldie reached up and grabbed the wrap that was draped around my neck. "Is dat mine?"

I nodded. "I was bringing it to you."

"Ah dat is so dweet."

"You probably should rest your mouth."

She spun around toward the house, but turned much too quickly because she started to fall backwards. I reached out just as she landed in my arms. I scooped her up, and her smooth, silky pink pajamas slide against my skin teasing my senses. Her long, golden locks fell over my arm awakening dormant desires. Her pajamas weren't like anything I'd ever seen. They were tailored with a button-up top that strained to conceal breasts that gently hung to reveal their natural slope and size that were generous. But it wasn't just that her breasts were ample. Her nipples rose in the night air and poked through the sexy, lace trim along her pajama top, arousing a want that stirred my imagination to unbutton her blouse with my mouth. Tucked in my arms, her drawstring pants hung low on her hips. These were as fitted as they were fine. Sweet dreams began and ended with what Goldie Locks wore to bed.

"I can walk," she said looking up at me.

The flecks of gold in her green eyes shone brightly in the moonlight. I knew who to thank for casting a late night beam on the beauty I held in my arms, but instead of acknowledging the man in the moon I stared down into her fair face and raised an eyebrow.

"Let you walk? And miss the chance to show off?" I shook my head. "Not gonna happen."

She giggled and leaned her head against my chest. For a fleeting moment, I felt like her hero and not the guy that accidentally gave her a right cross to the chin. I carried her over the threshold in my arms and toward the couch in the front room.

I wasn't going to be like my brother, Dylan, and test out all the beds to find the one that was the perfect fit. I wasn't going to do that for the simple fact that I wasn't sure where the bedrooms were. Her house may look like Dylan's, but its interior layout was nothing like his. And I wasn't about to traipse around the house with Goldie in my arms and risk hitting her head against a sharp corner or bang her into a bedpost. From the looks of her lip that had now tripled in size, I had already given her the Muhammad Ali of all hits. I needed to make sure she was okay and leave before I did any more damage to her or her home. As much as I wanted Goldie, and I did, her safety and wellbeing were more important than my carnal desire to slip off her pajamas and discover if Goldie was golden throughout.

The couch was positioned next to the fireplace. A protective glass shield revealed a small stack of firewood crisscrossed in the hearth just waiting for a match. I gently laid Goldie against a decorative pillow before making my way to the mantle where I palmed the painted white brick until I found the box of matches. The fire lit immediately, and Goldie was by my side.

"You should be resting," I said.

She rolled her eyes and pointed toward the kitchen with her index finger while she cupped her jaw with her hand.

"Ice?" I said.

She shook her mane of golden hair. "Nah," she said. "Chicken ingers and ies."

"Oh, ho, ho. I already ran that errand of chicken fingers and fries, but if that's what you want, I'd gladly go out and get you some. I've already ruined two of your dinners."

She held up her hand like a stop sign and placed her other hand on her narrow hip. Her draw-string pajama pants dipped to reveal her slender hip bone and the curve of her belly. She looked like a crossing guard with her outstretched hand in front of me. I wanted to pull her toward me and break all sorts of laws.

Goldie stared at me intently and drew in her bottom lip. I wasn't sure why she did it until she spoke, and then her speech was near perfect and it made me smile.

"Hay-wen, sell that story to one of those Grimm Brothers who may actually buy your fairy tale. I won't. I know *you* didn't eat my dinner. Your date did."

I cringed and tilted my head. "Yeah, well, she was my responsibility."

Goldie chuckled and then sucked in her lower lip again before she spoke, and it was sexy as hell. "Anastasia was a handful."

"Little bit." Just hearing her name was enough to make my dick shrivel. "So ice?"

Goldie's smile was enough to bring my cock back to life. "Yes, please."

I returned with a bag full of ice and two very full glasses of honey pot wine. Goldie held the glasses and nodded toward the hall closet. I opened it to find a large, thick, plaid blanket. She patted the floor in front of the fire. Again, she drew in her bottom lip.

"Don't Bears like picnics?"

"Yeah and picnic baskets, honey, rangers, I've heard them all." I shook out the blanket until it covered a good section of carpet in front of the fire that glowed before us.

Goldie sat with her legs crisscrossed just like the stack of firewood, and I sat opposite her. She handed me my wine glass, and I tilted it toward hers.

"To mistaken homes, mismanaged meals, and mishaps at midnight," I said.

She threw her head back and laughed. Her beautiful, swollen lips curved into a smile. "To better endings." Our glasses briefly chimed against one another.

When she drank, wine dripped down her chin. I leaned over and gently dabbed the streak from her face. "Should I take you to the ER?"

She shook her head. "Trauma."

"The trauma unit?" My voice sounded as hysterical as I suddenly felt.

She grinned and sucked in her bottom lip. "Swollen lips are typically caused by trauma to the mouth."

"I didn't mean to, you know, punch you. I was aiming for the door."

"Well, if you can't share a concussion with your loved one, what can you share?"

"I caused a concussion?" My tone had moved from hysterical to frenzied.

Goldie erupted into laughter. She held her side and started to sway again. Her honey-colored wine sloshed back and forth in her goblet like liquid gold.

"Are you all right?" I said and nervously laughed, which only made her laugh harder. "You don't really have a concussion, do you?"

She held her glass toward me. I quickly placed my glass on the ledge of the fireplace and grabbed hers. As soon as she was free of her wineglass, she leaned over and broke out into, what could only be described as a fit of giggles.

"Yeah, okay, I get it." I placed her glass on the fire place beside mine. "Ha. Ha. Ha. Very funny. Make fun of the guy who punched you. Nice."

At that comment, she only laughed harder. She stopped momentarily to point her finger at me and widen her beautiful green eyes. "You did! You punched me!"

I shook my head. "It was an accident."

But more laughter ensued. She barely came up for air when she looked at me with her purple, bruised lips, and then I began laughing. "I'm sorry," I said. "But those lips. Not so sexy."

She leaned over and looked at her reflection in the glass fireplace screen and howled. "Oh, my gosh! I look awful!"

"I know! You do!"

She leaned into me, and I leaned against her until we were laughing so hard we collapsed back on the blanket. We could barely breathe. With our hands on our stomachs, trying to catch our breath the fire warmed my feet and Goldie's laughter still seemed to echo in my ears.

"Well, this was probably the *worst* date night of my life," I said staring at the high ceiling in her house that looked like pixie dust had been scattered across it. It sparkled and shone like stars in the evening sky.

Everything in Goldie's house was magical.

Goldie elbowed me. "Ah, get over it, Bear. This was a *great* night. How many times do you get to hit on your brother's date?" She elbowed me again—only harder. "I mean, literally."

"Ah, thanks, Locks." I turned my head to her. "Didn't think I could feel any *worse* about my night." But she was grinning so wildly it was devastatingly cute. I shook my head and rolled my eyes for good measure.

She leaned over and kissed me quickly.

I playfully wiped my mouth with the sleeve of my shirt. "Ew, get those big lips off me."

She attempted to swat my arm, but I grabbed her wrist before she made contact. I raised an eyebrow. "Gotta be faster than that, Goldie. Us Bears are quick when we smell honey." I leaned toward her and started flirtatiously sniffing her neck. Her head turned toward my nose.

"Oh, that tickles." She wiggled beside me.

"This?" I said coyly panting and snorting like a big bear. She twisted and giggled, but couldn't get away because I still held her wrist. I continued to huff and puff like a hungry bear, but the smell of nectar on her neck, the warmth of her skin against mine, and the fire crackling and snapping before us was like a hot command for passion. All the elements were in place including my desire that drove my mouth to nibble her delicate earlobe.

She stopped squirming beside me and started turning into me. "Oh, Hayden."

My tongue trailed her earlobe down her neck. I softly kissed the hollow of her collarbone and gently buried my nose in the warmth richness of her hair that awakened my senses and my appetite. Goldie's hair smelled like raspberries and champagne.

"I don't know what you bathe in," I said with my

mouth pressed against the tender nape of her neck and my hand still wrapped around her wrist, pinning her to the blanket. "But I want to immerse myself in you."

I didn't even think before I spoke, and suddenly I wished I hadn't. I closed my eyes tightly. But then she stirred beside me.

"If you like how I smell, imagine how I taste."

I think I stopped breathing. *Game on.*

I slowly made my way to the opening of her silky pajamas. She arched toward me, and her cleavage sprang my cock to life. My mouth didn't wait to see if it could unbutton the top button. I held her wrist with one hand and tried to unbutton her top with the other, but the buttons were small and my coordination with one hand wasn't that great. I started to let go of her wrist when she shook her head.

"No," she said. "Rip it."

I tore her top open. Her golden locks covered some of her breasts, and it was pure visual eye candy. Her breasts were fair like her skin with dusty nipples that were large, succulent, and perfect. I bent over and pulled one in mouth. I was rewarded with a low moan. I used my free hand to hold the other breast and feel its full swell and slope. It hung in my hand like it belonged there. I circled her areola and teased her nipple with my thumb while my tongue pulled her other nipple in and out slowly. She softly moaned and raised her hips toward me. With her free hand, she reached for my pants, but I stopped her.

I gently released her breast and pinned her other hand above her head until she was my captive. I looked down at her and studied her face.

"How's your lip?" I gauged the puffiness. "The swelling's decreased. But how do you feel?"

She tilted her head. "It's kind of an odd time to be

asking this. Don't you think?"

With my hands covering her wrists and her breasts exposed for my viewing pleasure, I coyly smiled. "No, actually." I leaned over and licked her nipple. "I think now is the perfect time to assess your injuries." I smiled at the ease of my hospital-speak I used for her benefit. I slowly traced her areola with my tongue and flicked it across her nipple back and forth until it stood at attention.

"Your nipples, along with your breasts, are magnificently sized," I said admiringly and then looked up at her. "But if you're still injured, and you kind of are, I could spend an entire evening arousing every part of your body and all you have to do is lay back and…" I shrugged. "Simply enjoy the ride … without actually having to ride."

She slightly giggled. "But, Hayden, what if I want to ride?"

I removed my hand from her wrist for a brief second to wipe my face with my hand. "As much as I'd like to take you for a ride—and trust me I would," I rubbed the stubble on my chin as I spoke, "I don't have any condoms. I was just on a mission to return your scarf and bring you dinner."

She smiled. "So instead I get dessert?"

I nodded with a grin. "Exactly." I looked down at her sternly. "But," I said firmly and wagged my finger at her. "Since dessert is *my* treat, you have to allow *me* to serve *you*."

I repositioned my hand over her wrist and with her hands pinned beneath me, she looked up and slowly, seductively agreed. I returned my attention and my mouth to her luscious breasts. They were so generous and her cleavage so tight, I knew my cock belonged between them. I may not be able to be fully enjoy Goldie, but there was a lot of Goldie I could still savor. Besides the night was young, and there was a lot of Goldie Locks for this Bear to discover.

I released one of her wrists so that I could make my way toward her drawstring pants when suddenly her hand was on my belt. She unbuckled it, unbuttoned and unzipped my jeans within a matter of seconds. Startled, I looked up at her.

"ER nurse. Used to getting clothes off someone quickly and urgently in cases of an emergency."

I raised an eyebrow and released her nipple. "And what's the emergency, Nurse Lock?"

"We've got to get your cock between my tits, stat!"

I slowly wagged my free finger. "This is *my* dessert tray. I'll serve the treats when I'm good and ready."

Goldie dipped her hand beneath my boxer briefs and tugged tightly on my cock. "But I'm thinking you are good and ready." The wanton look in her greenish-gold eyes was enough to make me lose sight of the fact that I was the one driving this dessert train. Part of me wanted to release the bear within me and let it ride between her bounty of breasts until I lost my load all over her supple skin, but this wasn't about me tonight. *Come on, Hayden, focus.*

"Don't make me take away your hand privilege," I said sternly enough that she took a few last strokes of my cock before releasing her grip and slowly removing her hand.

Tease.

"Thank you," I said as if I wasn't aware of her game. As soon as her hand was back at her side, I pulled it up over her head and clamped my hand over her wrist.

"Hey!" She squealed. "I obeyed."

I shrugged. "Yeah, well, it's still my dessert, and I decide when you get to taste a sample. You sampled early." I lightly applied more pressure to her wrist. "There's always a penalty for sampling early." Goldie was pinned, and from the gleam in her eye she liked it.

I kicked off one of my boots and tossed it behind me and then the other. Getting my shirt off was going to be tricky without the use of my hands. I needed something to temporarily tie Goldie up, if even for no other reason than show. I looked around her living room. There weren't any loose threads hanging from her curtains, or tie-backs holding the curtains away from the wall, or rubber-banded rolled up newspapers scattered along the entry hallway. Even after crashing through her window, everything was in order. I scanned the front door to the foyer back to the fireplace. The entire front room was immaculate.

"Your house is sterile enough to operate in," I mumbled.

She giggled. "What are you looking for? Besides a condom," she said and started laughing.

I exhaled loudly and pressed down on her wrists. "We are *not* starting *that* up again. Unless…" I started to lift my weight off her. "You want me to leave and take dessert home with me? I'm not against having dessert alone."

She straightened her posture beneath me, and her breasts practically stood at attention. Goldie was sexy and adorable at the same time. "Tell me what you need and perhaps I could help?"

"Sometime to tie you up with, my dear."

She grinned. "How about your belt?"

"Beautiful *and* resourceful. Hmm. Who knew?" But then I hesitated.

"You still don't know how to get your belt

without releasing me, do you?"

"Pretty much."

"May I?" She looked up at me. "I promise not to spoil my appetite. I'll just get the belt."

"Fair enough."

I released Goldie's slender hand, and she slipped down and had my belt in her hand before I knew it was off my jeans.

"ER nurses? And here I was always dating princesses and their wicked stepsisters."

Even though I was supposed to use the belt to tie her up, when she reached behind me and pulled my shirt out my jeans, I instinctively ducked so she could pull my shirt over my head. I let go of her other wrist for a brief moment and lifted off the blanket in a one-arm pushup, but unlike when I came crashing through her front window and landed in this position, this time I looked impressive with my bare chest on display. This time she smiled. This time, she noticed.

Goldie placed her hands above her head. I used my belt to tie them loosely together before I stood above her bare-chested with my jeans open and my cock about to spring free.

Game time.

With my jeans off, I touched the tip of my cock and brought a drop of pre-cum to her lips. She licked my finger, and the flecks of gold in her eyes asked for more. I cinched the belt strap around her wrists, and she gasped.

"If you don't like how I serve dessert…"

She shook her head.

I held onto the strap like a long lead rope with Goldie as my captive. I slightly lifted her head and brought my cock to her mouth.

"Lick it."

Surprise and excitement filled her face.

"Gently. Don't suck it. Or I'll take it away. But lick it. Long, slow, meaningful licks. Make it worth my while or I leave."

Her tongue was the same color as her dusty nipples. I carefully placed the tip of my cock against her mouth, and her tongue roved over the deep, hard ridges of my cock with an insatiable hunger. I never allowed my cock to make contact with her lower lip, and it only heightened the pleasure. The more I had to contain her oral engagement around my cock, the more I spurted small spurts of cum in her mouth.

"Samples," I said before withdrawing my cock slick with her saliva and my cum. I softly lay her head back down on the blanket, but kept tension on her wrists. Goldie looked up at me for the next play. I wielded total control. It was foreign, and I knew from the spark of desire she liked it.

I held onto the lead rope and knelt down beside her with my cock aimed toward her breasts.

"Time for dessert?"

She nodded.

Holding the lead rope in one hand, I carefully straddled her so that my wet cock was sandwiched between her milky breasts, and I would soon be buried between her legs. I pulled on the drawstring, and her pants slid off her long, tapered, toned legs.

Goldie wasn't golden blonde or white blonde. When it came to the nether regions Goldie's hair was the color of a lush, ripe strawberry. But it wasn't just her patch of strawberry hair that drew me to her sweetness. Goldie's hair was shaped into a heart that began above her clit and ended at her clit. It was as if Cupid himself were directing every lover, or at least the right lover, to the treasure trove itself. I leaned over and took a long, slow savory lick. She tasted like champagne.

I looked over my shoulder and tugged on the belt strap to gather her attention, though I didn't need to. Her eyes were already on me or my ass. I wasn't quite sure.

"You do taste better than you smell."

She raised her heart toward me. "You're not finished, are you?"

"Did I *say* I was finished?" I reached down between my legs and positioned my cock in the center of her breasts and started to slowly gyrate back and forth finding a rhythm that I took to her strawberry heart.

While I was rocking things back and forth, Goldie used the sides of my thighs as leverage to arch toward me, and if it was at all possible her breasts got larger. My cock slid between her breasts and created a suction that felt almost as good as the real thing.

Goldie's hands remained tied behind her head. As I slid my tongue along her clit and buried my mouth inside her, she instinctively arched, pulling her arms back and me almost along with her. It became a push and pull. And the more she pulled back, the more I had to pull forward to keep my mouth on her, my cock buried between her breasts and both of us on course to climax.

It was rough without being violent. The belt stretched so far between us it snapped and chafed skin. With my cock cushioned between her velvety full breasts, her nipples rubbed against my thighs. My tongue gained momentum against her clit as the rhythm of my cock increased. My body was completely working in tandem. Goldie purred beneath me.

"Hayden, don't stop," she said in a low, breathy voice.

Her thighs began to tremble, and her body began to shake. The amount of cum that started to ooze from my cock and lather between her breasts created greater force between us. I drove my cock between her breasts as if I was thrusting myself into her. My mouth plunged into her wetness with the craving of man that wanted to please a woman, and I did. More than anything I wanted to bring that golden goddess to ecstasy.

Somehow she worked her breasts in rapid succession up and down over my cock in a manner that could only be described as divine. My mind and body shut down, and she controlled my cock. I no longer did.

I wanted to see her. But instead I tasted her. I ate and drank the sweet nectar that exploded from her when she arched her back for the final time and released an explosion of flavor in my mouth. Her voice raised toward the sparkled ceiling that I imagined had parted and opened to the sky, and even the man in the moon was envious of the siren cry, the euphoria Goldie emitted when ecstasy was hers.

Hearing her climax, my thighs tightened, my hand clamped down on her thighs as my cock exploded between her breasts. My hand released the lead rope, and I gently slid off her. I moved up toward her. Her dusty nipples had turned crimson, beads of sweat had collected on the swell of her breasts, and she collapsed against my chest. I gently pushed the hair off her face and kissed her bottom lip that fortunately wasn't nearly as swollen.

"Since I still owe you dinner, how about I make it up with breakfast? I make the most amazing pumpkin spice pancakes you will *ever* taste. Combined with maple honey syrup." I slightly elbowed her. "I don't want to brag, but I've been told it's better than anything Hansel *or* Gretel offer for brunch."

She smiled and kissed me. "I have to work in a few hours."

I leaned my head against hers. "Goldie, no. Call in sick. Tell them you were punched by some beast. I am a Bear. It's not too far from the truth."

She giggled against me. "Rain check?"

"Is that a joke?"

She laughed again.

I was about to kiss her when there was a loud, clearly audible knock on the front door. I glanced at my watch. It was three in the morning. "What the hell?" I looked at the door and then back at Goldie. "Is that your ride to work or something?"

Her cheeks suddenly tinged with heat. "Crap."

"What?"

"I think it's your brother, Dylan."

Chapter Six

"So how was your date?"

I held up my finger and wagged it like a dog's tail. "Nuh-uh. First you've got to tell me about your hair. What the heck, Rapunzel? Are those like seven feet extensions?"

Her hair was a lighter shade of blonde than mine, almost white-blonde, and hung past her waist and swung like a thick rope. There wasn't a man in The Enchanted Forest tavern that wasn't checking her out.

"Do you like it?" She glanced over her shoulder. "It almost touches the floor!"

"Do I like it?" I squealed with her. "It's fantabulous. But seriously how long is it?"

She shrugged. "At least four feet. I wanted something different. It's bad enough I'm stuck in that ivory tower all day with only one window to look out and scarcely a visitor to come see me."

"The life of an academic can't be easy," I said.

"I just didn't think it would be this lonely."

"Maybe you're just *so* intellectual that no one else feels smart enough to come up to your office in the tower and problem-solve with you," I said.

Rapunzel purposefully shook her head so her new, longer locks would be the envy of everyone in The Enchanted Forest, academic or not.

I elbowed her. "See, that's the spirit. Besides, if your new hair doesn't get someone up to that tower, I'm not sure what will. Though," I said and lifted my martini glass toward her, "your hair is so long now you could just toss it out the window of your office and let some man climb up to you."

She raised her glass and gently clinked it against mine. "To discovering new ways of meeting men."

We both took a long, slow sip of our Appletini.

"Oh, that's yummy," I said.

"Yeah, Doc hired a new bartender, Snow something, and that girl can mix up a martini. Apples are her specialty. It's her poison."

"Right." I took another sip and slowly glanced around the tavern. It was hopping for a Wednesday night. "Where's Ariel? I thought she was meeting us, too?"

"Oh, yeah, I meant to tell you. She texted that her boss, Sebastian, was keeping her at work and she'd be running late. Apparently the guy's a real crab," Rapunzel said.

"Bummer. I always like our weekly get-together. Same bar, same barstool, it's our thing." I placed my martini glass down on the bar with a little too much force.

Doc looked at me from the other end of the bar and shook his head.

"Sorry," I said in his direction and then leaned toward my bestie and spoke under my breath. "And I thought his brother Grumpy was hard to deal with. Sheesh."

"Okay, little miss redirect," Rapunzel said. "You're not getting out of spilling the beans about your date with Mr. Honey Pot wine … what's his name again?"

"Dylan."

"Oh, that bad, huh?"

"What?" I raised my shoulders and my eyebrows defensively.

"The drop in your voice? I thought you were excited about this Bear guy."

I drew a deep breath. "I was excited," I lowered both my shoulders and my eyebrows. "I mean I *am* excited about this Bear guy, but then—" I exhaled and looked at my friend. "Everything's a mess."

"Oh, no, what happened? Didn't he take you to The Magic Oven? I hear that place is redonkulously romantic."

I titled my head toward the ceiling in the tavern that was lit by candle chandeliers and wondered what it would be to have a drink with Hayden beneath the fire's flame. "Wrong brother," I said.

"What?"

I lowered my head, and Rapunzel pushed my hair off my shoulder. "Dylan took me to The Magic Oven. He was the one I came home to find asleep in my bed. But then his brother, Hayden, showed up and interviewed us for the radio station, and there was this chemistry between us…"

"And…"

"But Dylan asked me out on the date, so I went out to dinner with Dylan and it was nice." I grimaced when I meant to smile.

"That bad, huh?"

"Worse."

"Hayden, I mean—" Again I shook my head. "*Dylan* was super nice, but…" Hayden's face surfaced in my mind, and I broke out laughing.

"So was it bad funny? Or…"

"No, I was just thinking of something Hayden did."

"The one that interviewed you?"

"Yeah, and the one that *pretended* to wolf down my dinner. Anyway, Hayden was on this date with another woman at another table, and it didn't look like it was going well." I fanned the air with my hand so the image of him and Anastasia would hopefully evaporate. "I'm not sure *what* exactly happened, but Hayden ended up buying us a second supper because he said he ate ours."

Now Rapunzel shook her finger. "What? First his brother ends up lying in your bed and then the second brother resorts to eating off your plate? Goldie Locks, who are these Bears?"

I weighed her comments in the palms of my hands like a scale. "Yeah, that's the thing. Dylan did sleep in my bed." My palm shot down low in his favor. "But Hayden…" My palm remained stationary. "His date had more Raclette on the side of her mouth, and he didn't have any cheese on his face. I *know* he didn't eat *any* of my food. He was—"

"Being a gentleman and covering for her?"

"Exactly." My palm and the scales in Hayden's favor rose high in the air. "But it doesn't matter now." I exhaled, dropped my hands and twirled my finger in what was left of my green-tinted drink.

"Uh, Why? If Hayden did that to help his date save face, he's one of the good guys." Rapunzel held up her finger toward the dark-haired bartender.

The new bartender approached us. Her skin was alabaster and her eyes a piercing blue. "Another Appletini?" she said.

We both nodded and answered. "Yes, please."

"Okay," Rapunzel said. "We've established that Hayden's a good guy and your face lights up when you talk about him, so I'm not seeing a downside."

I tilted my head, and my chest rose and fell with gentle, stirring thoughts about Hayden. "And he's such an amazing lover."

Rapunzel was polishing off the last of her Appletini when she practically spit it out. Instead, she swallowed hard and looked at me even harder. "What?"

I shrugged. "Didn't I mention that we ended up together after my date with his brother went south?"

Four feet of hair shook at me like a wavering flag of protest. "Uh, Goldie, I would have remembered that detail." She reached over, grabbed my wrist, and I winced. I tried to pull away when Rapunzel pushed up the sleeve of my black jacket. "What the hell? Are those rope burns?"

I cringed and pulled my arm away and tucked my wrist back under the sleeve of my jacket. "More like … belt burns."

"Goldie Locks!" Rapunzel slapped the bar's countertop. Grumpy shook his head at her. "Ah, settle down. This is a bar. If you wanted to run a quiet establishment, you should have bought a library."

"Shh!" I giggled. "I don't want Grumpy or Doc or any of the seven wonders who own this place to kick us out. Or worse, know the details of…"

"Belt burns?"

I glanced up again at the chandeliers and then back at Rapunzel. "Maybe?"

"Where was Dylan when all this was happening?"

"Well that's the thing," I said.

Rapunzel leaned in like I was about to tell her a juicy secret, which wasn't too far off the mark. "Was Dylan part of this, too?"

I slowly shook my head. "No!" I almost burst out laughing. Instead I swatted her and wished I hadn't. "Oh, ow."

"Really."

I rolled my eyes. "My wrists are still tender, and any contact is a painful reminder of something I'm sure I'll *never* experience again."

The bartender placed two fresh Appletinis between us. I quickly finished the remnants of my first and slid the glass toward her with a smile. I reached for the delicious apple-flavored, alcohol-induced treat and brought it to my lips.

"Okay so what *exactly* happened?" Again Rapunzel closed in the space between us clearly not wanting to miss any details.

But first I took a long slow, savory sip. I needed liquid courage to tell my best friend how I had let the absolute best guy slip through my fingers.

"Suffice to say, ever since that night I now carry condoms with me." I patted my purse that hung on the back of my barstool. "And let's just say that Hayden knows his way around the human anatomy, I'll *never* look at a man's belt the same way again, and as far as Bears go…" I inhaled and I swear his spicy scent rose through my nose and tickled my senses. "Hayden's not too big. Not too small, he's *just right*."

Rapunzel lightly clapped her hands together. "Oh, Goldie, I'm so happy for you!"

I slowly shook my head. "No. Don't be."

"Why? What gives?"

"Dylan gives. He showed up just when things were winding down between me and Hayden."

Rapunzel elbowed me so hard I almost fell off my barstool. "Nuh-uh. No, he didn't!"

I gritted a smile. "But oh he did."

"Why?"

"I kind of invited him over?"

My friend held her face like the kid in the *Home Alone* movies and looked as horrified. "Who does that?"

"Well, I didn't expect to end up in bed with his brother!" I said a bit too loudly. "Dylan's a good guy, too, but he was so nervous. But once I got him to relax, he's just, I don't know, he's fun to be around. He's sweet and nice, so I thought that maybe he could come over before I went to work and we could have coffee together?"

"At what three in the morning?"

I cringed. "Yeah, I didn't really think it through. It was one of those moments when you're saying goodnight to someone and it's really awkward and you just want to get out of the car and into your house, so you kind of say anything." I looked at my friend for confirmation, but all she did was shake her long new mane of hair.

"You just get out of the car and go into your house."

I exhaled loudly. "Don't be so academic. That's why you don't have any dates." I tried changing the topic. "You're too rational."

She slowly shook her index finger at me. "Not going to fly. You asked Dylan *back* to your house for coffee at three in the morning before the start of your shift."

"Yeah, I was moving back to mornings, and I thought it'd be fun to, I dunno, have coffee with him?"

"So he shows up when Hayden's still there?"

I closed my eyes and tried to erase the memory.

"Oh. My. God." Rapunzel elbowed me to wake me back up to reality. "What happened?"

"Before or after Hayden grabbed his clothes, looked at me in disgust, and took off through my back door?"

Rapunzel leaned back against her bar stool. "Wow."

I slowly, painfully nodded and took another long sip of my Appletini. "I did text him," I said with my head practically in the martini glass. "Hayden, I mean. I texted him when Dylan was fumbling around with my coffee maker. I tried to explain to him that I had just invited his brother over for coffee and nothing more, but…"

"Let me guess, your cell phone went dark and silent?"

I nodded. "How long do you think he'll stay mad?" I held onto my glass and looked at Rapunzel. She had a nice rosy, pink tint to her cheeks. Or maybe it was my frosted glass. It was hard to tell. "Do you think this is irreversible damage? Or do you think maybe after a little time he'll come around?"

She gently rubbed my shoulder. "I don't know because I don't know him. But most guys…"

Her voice trailed off. I didn't have to hear her finish the sentence to know that most guys wouldn't be all right if another guy, especially their brother, showed up at a woman's house at three in the morning.

"Did he try to kiss you? Dylan, I mean, in the morning?"

"Oh, hell no. I mean there's nothing wrong with him, but he's just kind of…" I couldn't put my tongue on the right word.

"Passive?" His voice came from behind me.

Startled, I jumped. Rapunzel did, too, but then she yelped. "My hair! It's stuck."

I jumped off my barstool and gently released her hair that had wrapped around the wooden spindles of her chair.

The man stood closely beside me. Too close. He towered above me with massive shoulders and a wide frame. He was one bear of a man and definitely encroaching on my bubble.

"Do you mind?" I said to him. "You already scared me and my friend. I think giving us a little room would be nice." Working the ER, I had learned the necessity of space and how to get it.

He held up his hands in mock protest. They looked less like hands and more like padded mitts. The guy was seriously massive. "Sorry," he said. "Here I was thinking I was helping. I overheard you bellyaching about some passive puss in boots that couldn't seem to get his act together, so I thought I'd jump into the conversation and show you how a man, who isn't afraid of women, acts."

I rolled my eyes at Rapunzel. She raised an eyebrow toward me and mouthed, "He's kind of cute." This only made me give her a longer exasperated eye roll.

"Can we start over?" he said and plopped down in my barstool.

"Excuse me? You're sitting on my stool?"

"Does it have your name on it?" He slapped the bar and started laughing. His breath reeked of apples.

"Okay, I think someone's had one too many Appletinis," I said.

He held up his hand. "Listen, Goldie."

"How did you know my name?"

"I didn't. Lucky guess." He again slapped the bar with his hand. "Hey, Snowy, send me another apple shot. Make it two." He held up three fingers.

I shook my head and looked at the end of the bar for Doc or Grumpy or any of the seven wonders that owned The Enchanted Forest, but of course, none of them were anywhere to be seen. *Stupid little men.*

"Listen, I just want my barstool back," I said. "It's where we always sit on Wednesday. It's just our thing. So if you wouldn't mind…"

"Oh, so this is *your* barstool?" The man slowly shook his head. "I bet you're some rich snob from the East side."

My face must have revealed that I lived on the East side.

"You are, aren't you? Classic. You snotty little Eastsiders think *everything* in Amāre belongs to you. Yeah, well, it doesn't."

"I just want to sit back down," I said gently. "My drink is on the bar and…"

"You just want your barstool back, is that it?" His apple-liquored breath dripped with contempt.

"Yes, please," I said.

"Well I just want my bar back. This used to be The Golden Goose tavern until the owner got a winning lottery ticket, hit the jackpot with three golden eggs in a row, cashed out and took his winnings to the East side. This used to be a place where locals from all around Amāre could come and feel welcome. Now it's just a hot spot for Easties to spend their money on specialty fruity drinks. So before this was *your* barstool, it belonged to me."

"I'm sorry," I said. "I didn't know the history."

"No, of course not. You're too busy worrying about *your* barstool."

"I know it's not mine. I just sit there once a week when my girlfriends and I come out for a drink." I nervously laughed. "It just *feels* like it's my barstool."

"Well, geez then I better hurry. I'm just a hardworking man from the Westside, but if the lady wants her barstool back…" The man slowly raised himself off the barstool, using the bar top as leverage. He reached behind him, grabbed the wood spindles that formed the back of the bar stool, lifted the entire chair over his head and smacked it against the bar. Wood splinters flew through the air.

Rapunzel screamed, but I was too busy ducking and covering my head to utter a word.

"Westsiders, it's time to take back the bar." The man charged toward the center of the crowd.

I grabbed Rapunzel's hand and tried to make it toward the front entrance, but the room started to spin. I looked at the new bartender, who was happily eyeing the man that had just started the brawl and realized there was more to her Appletini than met the eye.

Chapter Seven

"Hayden, I think we've got a fifty-one-fifty at The Enchanted Forest," Bob bellowed above the drone of reporters hitting the keys on their laptops.

"Ah, fifty-one-fifty, classic Van Halen song," I said.

"Hayden, it's no joke or time for musical references."

"A fifty-one-fifty? That's police code for crazy and insane. Or something like that," I said.

"Just heard it over the scanner that the Amāre police have a possible fifty-one-fifty at The Enchanted Forest." Bob tossed me the keys to the news van. "They're holding some guy, a big guy, by the sounds of it because he went a bit crazy in the tavern."

"The Enchanted Forest?" I shook my head. "That's upscale now. There hasn't been a bar fight in Amāre since Goose owned the tavern."

"Well the times they are a-changing, my friend," my editor said citing his own taste in music. "Now get to The Enchanted Forest and get there fast. I want live interviews. Sounds like there were some women that got caught in the crossfire."

I headed toward the radio station parking lot.

"And don't forget the brawler. I'd like to get him on tape, too," Bob called out.

I nodded and wondered what awaited me. It had to be a lot better than the last twenty-four hours. No matter how many times I reread Goldie's text I just couldn't get the image or sound of Dylan pounding on her door out of my mind. I wasn't sure if it was because he knocked so loud when I had punched the door, or rather Goldie, or if it was because he was even there. I knew Dylan was no threat to what Goldie and I had shared. I just wasn't willing to let go of what tore at my gut. I felt betrayed. I don't know why, but I did. It was silly because I barely knew Goldie, but I already knew she was the type of person that would welcome Black Beard himself into her house and offer him shelter if he needed it. She was a nurse. It was just how she was hardwired. She cared. I just didn't like that she had once again cared for my older brother when I was the clearly the Bear for her. Coffee or not. Innocent or not.

I shook my head and tried to erase the images of her body from my mind. Or her smell from my senses. But she was permanently etched in my memory. I drove the news van fast and furiously to my next assignment. A bar fight was in perfect order.

The Enchanted Forest tavern wasn't actually in the forest, but rather on the outskirts of Amāre. While the cottage was charming with amber colored-roof shingles and slanted eaves where lanterns hung and lit the way for travelers, just beyond its reach, there wasn't anything enchanted about the dark forest. It was a place where even the most skilled huntsman wouldn't travel.

The sirens were silenced, but the lights on top of the trooper's SUVs swirled in the night air like a foreboding. I stepped inside the cottage that was beautifully decorated with ornate wood beams with woodland animals and hunters carved into the timber. From the barstools to the candle chandelier, The Enchanted Forest was a visual wonder.

"He was sitting on my barstool."

Her voice rose above the chatter and clatter of dishes and glasses being cleared away. I walked toward her golden hair that gently draped the shoulders of her black jacket. *What is she doing here?*

I was about to turn away when I noticed the rip on her black jacket, her hands shaking and her friend by her side. I rushed toward her.

"I just asked him was if I could have my barstool back," she said.

She turned as I approached.

"Hayden!" She wrapped her arms around me. "I'm so glad you're here."

Warmth flooded my body. "Are you okay?" I scanned her face and instinctively leaned in to kiss the top of her head and stopped. I looked at her. "Goldie, what happened?"

"Some guy had a bit too much to drink and ended up getting a tad territorial when I asked for my barstool back," she said.

"That's crazy. Where is this brute?"

"Hey, brother."

I hung my head and closed my eyes. *Camden.*

"Do you know him?" Goldie's voice rang high and tight in the tavern.

I opened my eyes and slowly nodded. "Yeah, afraid so." I turned away from her and in his direction. "Hey, Camden, how's my favorite little brother doing?"

"I'm your *only* little brother, so don't patronize me."

"He's *your* brother? And Dylan's too?" Goldie looked at me and him and back again at me.

"Yeah, why? Should I set up a date with him, too?"

Goldie's hand reached up and slapped my face faster than I could withdraw my comment.

"You're a real jerk." She turned to leave when Burt intercepted her.

"I'm sorry, Miss Locks, but I still have some questions I need you to answer."

She looked at me, and her green eyes didn't shine with flecks of gold. Nor were they alive with fire, passion, or even anger. When I looked at Goldie, her eyes were dull, flat, and sad. I had taken the one thing that I didn't think was possible from Goldie, her magic.

"Dude, you *are* a jerk."

The woman beside Goldie with extremely long, blonde hair snorted a laugh at my brother's comment. I turned sideways and stood between Goldie and my little brother. "Excuse me?" I said toward Camden.

"Bro, all night long she's been going on about this guy she's absolutely crazy about and his lame older brother who kept ruining it for her. I should have known it was Dylan." Camden shook his head. "But now you go and say something eff'd up like that? What's *your* problem?"

"What are you talking about?" I stared at my younger brother as if he'd grown a third eye.

"I mean that you're about as street smart as Dylan and about as savvy as Grumpy or Doc down there." Camden cocked his head toward the end of the bar.

I raised my shoulders and threw up my hands. "Still no idea what you're talking about."

"Okay, bro, how about this, you've got middle child, or in our case, middle Bear, issues."

I shook my head. "Camden, you're making absolutely no sense."

"What your brother is trying to tell you is that if you weren't so hung up on being noticed, you would have seen that Goldie liked you from the get-go. So your little insult, hell, your slam against my best friend, was completely uncalled for." The woman with ridiculously long hair stood in front of me and swung it back and forth. Despite my best efforts I couldn't stop staring at her hair that swayed behind her with the steady tempo of a metronome. Unfortunately her tone wasn't nearly as soothing. "Goldie was simply being Goldie. She asked Dylan back to her house for coffee. *Just coffee.* Nothing more, nothing less. She didn't ask him back to her house to hook up or be *belted* up for the night."

I felt my body temperature instantly spike and my cheeks ignite with heat. I didn't dare look at Goldie, but her friend grabbed Goldie's wrists and flashed them before me. They were red, chafed, and looked irritated.

Camden started laughing, and out of the corner of my eye I saw Burt shake his head.

"So maybe instead of accusing Goldie of wanting to date your other brother, maybe you should be considering your own actions and seriously kissing the ground she walks on because there's not many woman in Amāre who'd let a man tie her up with his belt."

"True that," Camden said, and then fist-bumped the woman who finally stopped talking long enough for me to say something.

I turned to Goldie. "I did read your texts." I paused. *Should I hold her hands? No. Kiss her? No.* Instead, I looked into her eyes. "I'm really sorry for being…"

"Insecure?" Camden jumped into the conversation with Rapunzel quickly on his heels.

"Insensitive?" she said.

Goldie stepped up. "Enough."

Shocked, I took a step back.

"Listen." She turned to me. "Maybe you were a bit insecure and definitely insensitive. But—" She pivoted on the heel of her boot and looked at my brother and her friend. "*I'm* the one that invited Dylan over to my house for coffee after having gone out to dinner with him. What else was Hayden to think?"

I wasn't sure what to say. For a moment, I thought I saw a flicker of a smile cross Goldie's face, but if it did it just as quickly vanished. "I should have responded to your texts," I said, "and for certain I *never* should have made that comment. It was—" I grimaced, thinking that I had actually thrown my little brother in her face. "*I* was awful." I placed my hand on my chest. "I was out of line. You didn't deserve that. I hope you'll forgive me." She didn't say anything, and her eyes didn't waver.

I slowly nodded, and it felt like my heart plummeted to my stomach. *Understood.*

"Well, perhaps I could start over. Miss Locks, I'd like you to meet the youngest Bear, Camden. But that's it. Now you've met us all," I said at a weak attempt at humor. But Goldie neither smiled nor laughed.

I looked at Camden. "Cam, this is Miss Locks, and it sounds like maybe there was some incident here tonight that involved you and some barstool?" I tried to remain neutral balancing the scales between Goldie and Camden, but Camden was still my brother. I knew he was a hot-headed Bear, but he was family.

"Listen, Hayden, even though she's crazy about you, she's some rich Eastsider with too much time of her hands. I accidentally sat in her barstool, and she flipped out on me. I was defending myself."

If Camden's face wasn't so serious I would have laughed. Instead I said, "Camden, you're over six two and built like one of the Pig Brothers' brick houses. Goldie's got to be all of five foot nothing and at best weighs a buck twenty—wet. Now let's get real. What happened?"

Camden crossed his arms over his barrel chest.

"Cam, the scanner reported on a possible fifty-one-fifty. Do you know what that means?"

He remained silent.

"Well, little brother, what that means is that an officer, like Burt here," I looked over at my former college roommate. "Burt could involuntarily confine you to a hospital if they suspect you are a danger to yourself or others. And clearly," I fanned my arm around the tavern. "From the looks of things, you decided to defend the *entire* tavern. Now." I took a step closer to him. "Would you like to explain to me exactly what happened?"

Chapter Eight

I stood silently next to Hayden. I wasn't about to say anything because I wasn't sure what to say. Burt and Rapunzel were on the other side of me. We were all waiting for Camden to answer his brother's question.

"It was a mistake," Camden said flatly, curtly, and without apology. He was nothing like his brother, Hayden, and even further from the oldest Bear, Dylan. But Camden had defended me to Hayden. *What is it about little Bear?*

I looked at Hayden. He was visibly embarrassed by his brother's behavior, and worse he seemed befuddled as to what to do next.

"Clearly, it was a mistake," Hayden said. "But what exactly happened?"

Camden nodded toward a corner of the tavern. Hayden looked at Burt and then at me. "I think things could get resolved a lot faster and easier if I could talk to my brother privately."

I nodded and took a step back. "Of course."

Burt stepped into the conversation. "When the call came across the scanner I wondered if Cam had something to do with tonight's ruckus. I'm here on the Captain's orders with clear instructions to make sure the Bear brothers get their act together and leave Miss Locks alone."

I held up my hand as if we were in a school room and not a tavern. "Burt…"

"Yes, Miss Locks," he said.

I nodded. "I honestly don't think the Bear brothers are any danger to me. Or that they're targeting me. I think it's just been," I raised my shoulders to my ears, "a string of bad luck."

Hayden's dark, soulful eyes looked at me and smiled. "Thank you. May I still have a minute alone with my brother?"

The two Bears walked to a corner of the tavern. I looked around for Rapunzel. She was at the end of the bar. A man in a pricy suit with lacquered black hair and charming good looks was chatting her up. I smiled. *Maybe one of us is going to find our happily ever after.*

****

"Dude, what is wrong with you?" I stared at my brother.

He combed his fingers through his hair and exhaled loudly. "Listen, I'm not like you or Dylan."

"What do you mean?"

"Dylan's got the magic touch with trees. He can spot one and know it's got the best honey that he can spin into liquid gold. And you." My little brother pointed to me. "You're this popular radio jock with a honeyed voice that *everyone* loves. You could have any woman in Amāre."

I scoffed. "No, I can't. Nor do I want *every* woman." I glanced over my shoulder at Goldie. "I only want one."

My younger brother's chuckle made me turn back in his direction. "What?"

"Well, if you hadn't have been such an ass you may have been able to have Goldie."

"Maybe."

"Oh, you've got it bad for little Miss Locks," he said.

I lightly punched him on the shoulder. "Maybe I do, but nothing's going to happen if you don't get your act together and apologize for heisting her barstool."

"I kind of did a bit more than just heist it."

I tilted my head. "What did you do?"

"Well, I kind of broke it into little bits and pieces."

I drew a deep breath. "And *why* would you do that?"

Camden shrugged. "I had a few too many apple shots, and I let surface the age-old issue that always raises its head when I drink."

"The Eastside versus the Westside," I stated as fact.

"Yup, that's the one."

"Well, what are we going to do? The Golden Goose was sold to seven small businessmen that have a right to run it the way they deem fit. They can charge whatever they want and hire whomever they like. That's just life, little brother."

"They did hire one fine looking bartender." Camden cocked his head toward the bar.

I glanced again over my shoulder. "She's a bit pale for my taste, but if you like that translucent skin and dark hair…"

"Like it? I'm in love with it," Camden said.

"They why did you start a bar fight over a barstool? And Goldie's barstool no less."

"That fair little creature over there," Camden said. "She's a little minx with the drinkology. She can mix up one helluva drink. I was trying to show off by keeping up with her apple shots, but…"

"They got the better of you?"

Camden nodded.

"So the barstool?" I looked at my brother for clarity.

"That was the apples talking. I do get a bit territorial over the Eastside and Westside thing, but I really didn't mean any harm," he said. "Goldie just kind of got in the way."

"Got in the way?" I heard my voice rise, but I didn't care. Everyone had their breaking point. "Are you kidding me? She's amazing. She's beautiful. How does a woman like Goldie get in anyone's way? But thanks to you, Dylan, and my stupid, insensitive, careless remark she'll never want to get near any Bear again. I just lost the woman I love." I wiped my face with my hands, and when I looked back up, Goldie was standing beside me.

****

"In the emergency room, we get to know when a person is stressed out or on overload because of these little things they do that they might not normally do," I said.

Hayden grinned. "Oh-kay. Like a tell? Are you talking about tells? Because I'm the king of knowing someone's tell."

I playfully rolled my eyes. "Well, actually a tell is an unconscious action when a person is attempting to deceive someone, like in poker or chess." I gently touched his shoulder, and a wave of electricity rushed between us. I couldn't help but smile. My body reminded me that while I may try to deny my feelings, physical reactions couldn't be fooled.

"What I'm talking about," I said, "is body language. And someone's body language often reveals how that person is doing emotionally or mentally. It's a simple gesture or action, but it literally speaks volumes."

Hayden crossed his arms over his chest and practically shook my hand off him.

I giggled. "See that's one right there. Your body language is clearly closed off to this topic."

His laughter was rich and wonderful to hear. He reached for my hand and held it. "Okay, what's your point, blondie?"

I grinned widely. "I noticed at The Magic Oven that you wiped your face with your hand just before you had to rush to the kitchen to change your date's dinner order. Though," I looked at Hayden and raised an eyebrow, "I think Anastasia enjoyed my meal a lot more than her own."

Hayden's cheeks ignited in color, and he squeezed my hand. "We already established that I was just trying to do the right thing."

"It's fine! I'm playing with you," I said. "And I noticed that you wiped your face with your hand when we were alone at my house, and you realized you didn't have…" I didn't say condoms, but Hayden's face still turned a few shades of red as if I had. "You were concerned that you were letting me down. But you didn't, did you?"

He gently rubbed my wrists. "I don't know? Your friend seems to think that I hurt you, like I'm a beast."

"You are a beast." I smiled. "But it was one of the best nights of my life. And when you were talking with Camden, you *just* did the same gesture. You wiped your face with your hands, and it seems like you were talking about something that seems very important to you."

Hayden's brooding bedroom eyes were all that I could see. "It is very important to me."

"Well, I just want you to know," I took a step closer to him. "There's nothing that either of your brothers could do that would change how I feel about this Bear."

With our hands already interlocked, Hayden pulled me into him. I looked up into his eyes and smiled.

"What about Dylan?" he asked with his lips close to mine.

"Dylan's a wonderful man. But the oldest Bear is a bit too shy for me," I said.

"And Camden?" Hayden's voice teetered on panic.

I glanced over at his little brother and shook my head playfully. "Well, let's just say baby Bear is a bit too much for me."

Camden smiled.

"And me?" Hayden's voice was barely above a whisper. "Will you ever forgive me?"

"Oh, the middle Bear? The one that's not too shy or not too much? The one that seems to show up just when I need him? And sometimes says the wrong thing? That Bear brother?"

Hayden nodded.

"Even when he says the wrong thing, he knows how to make it right. And *that* makes this Bear," I said squeezing his hand, "just right."

Then the middle Bear brother kissed me. And in that kiss was the richness and promise of happily ever after.

Chapter Nine

In exchange for not pressing charges, the seven owners of The Enchanted Forest had agreed that if Camden replaced what he broke and cleaned the tavern he would also be allowed to come back and drink. And since Camden was still smitten with Snow the bartender, he gladly accepted the terms of the agreement.

"You shouldn't be doing this," Hayden said as he picked up a beer can and placed it in the rolling trash can I pushed toward him.

I pulled my hair back into a ponytail and shrugged. "Camden's coming off one too many apple shots, and I think Rapunzel wanted to drive him home."

Hayden looked up at me and smiled. "Really?"

I nodded. "Yeah."

He leaned against the trash can for a moment. "I could see that working."

"Me, too." Suddenly something hot hit the top of my hand. "What the hell!"

"What?"

I shook my hand.

"Is it your wrist?"

I shook my head, and then another fiery zap smacked down on my other hand. "Damn it! Hayden, help! It's got me!"

He rushed toward me. "What is it?" He looked around the tavern, but we were completely alone.

"Something hot keeps burning me," I said.

Hayden looked up, and I followed his gaze. The ceiling was still lit by candles from the many chandeliers stationed throughout the tavern. Since the bar fight, the tables had been repositioned, and now hot wax dripped down without a center place to land.

Hayden moved me aside before another drop of candle wax could fall upon me. Instead, his forearm took the hit.

"Damn that smarts!"

I giggled. "Right."

He rubbed his arm when I saw another bead of wax plunge toward him.

"Move!" I yelled.

Hayden charged me as he dove for cover. We landed under a large oak table. Tucked in his embrace, moisture rushed to my panties at the heat of his breath of my neck.

"I think we're safe here," he said.

I nodded.

"We seem to find ourselves in unusual situations," he said.

I tilted my head toward the underside of the oak table. "This?" I shrugged. "It's where Rapunzel and I always end up after a good round of drinking."

"Ah, but that's the problem. I haven't had anything to drink," Hayden said and exhaled. "And after a night like tonight…" He glanced toward the bar. "You think it's worth it?"

I slowly shook my head. "Tough call. If you do, you risk the wax. But if you don't, you forfeit not knowing *just* how good those Appletinis are." I shrugged. "Like I said, tough call."

He rubbed the stubble on his chin. "Excellent points. You think that bartender, Snow, still has a batch of spiced 'tinis back there?"

"Oh, I *know* she does."

He leaned his head dangerously close toward me like he was some rogue interrogator. His spicy scent filled the air between us. "Who's your source?"

I held up my hand. "I protect my sources. But he's reliable."

He snapped. "Camden! Only my brother would know if there was still more booze in this joint."

I giggled. "Maybe. Maybe not. But it is a bar."

Hayden rolled his eyes, pulled his black shirt out of his jeans, unbuttoned it and darted out from beneath the table with his shirt capped over his head like Dracula. I started to laugh, and as I watched him zigzag across the tavern toward the bar, I couldn't stop laughing and cheering him on simultaneously.

"Go! Go! Go! You're almost there!"

Instead of rounding the bar, he leapt over it. I shook my head, but it was nonetheless dramatic and sexy as hell.

I snuck my head out just in time to see him pop up from the bartender's position with a silver shaker in one hand and what looked like two chilled martini glasses in the other. I clapped.

"Go, Hayden!"

He rallied to the cry. "Comin', my lady!"

But without his shirt to shield his head, the wax was sure to get him. I cringed. *That's gonna burn.*

But somehow by either sheer determination or dumb luck, Hayden crisscrossed his way back beneath the table without getting zinged by any wax from the now many dripping chandeliers overflowing with hot wax.

"How do they turn those things off, anyway?" I said when he scooted in beside me.

"I'm sure Snow hefts one of the seven wonders up on her shoulders and they blow them out each night."

Hayden never failed to make me giggle. "You're probably right."

He handed me the martini glasses. I held one in each hand, and they were cool to the touch. "Oh, this is going to be so good."

Hayden shook the shaker of Appletinis vigorously, looking like a pro. He untwisted the cap, and the lime-green concoction poured out smoothly.

"So this is your poison?" He took his glass from me.

I raised my shoulders to my ears and felt my entire body light up. "Just wait and you'll understand why."

He gently tipped the rim of his V-shaped glass toward mine. "To swanky sipping."

I watched him take the first sip. His face puckered, and he quickly shook his head. "It's a bit tart."

"I think Snow uses a sweet-and-sour mix to mask the taste of the alcohol."

Hayden took another sip. His eyebrows furrowed, and his face pulled in like a balloon when it loses air. "What's wrong with the taste of alcohol?"

I leaned my head back and laughed. "The better quality the vodka, the better the 'tini. But I'm not thinking that any of the seven businessmen of this tavern are going to let Snow buy the good stuff so she uses cheap vodka."

Hayden held the glass toward me. "You want mine?"

I shook my head. "Oh, no. Once an Appletini is started it must be finished."

He rolled his eyes. "Let me guess, something you and Rapunzel created?"

"No, it's just bad luck to not finish your drink."

When Hayden laughed, his delicious bare chest, which was fully on display, shook, and his toned, muscular six-pack looked better than anything, anywhere.

"Bad luck?"

I tilted my head. "You don't know. Maybe it is."

Hayden threw back the rest of his Appletini and slapped his thigh. "Damn! That is some bad shit." He took his glass, reached out from beneath the table and set it on top. "Good thing you and your girlfriends like that drink because there's no man in Amāre that'll drink that."

I smiled, and my voice suddenly softened. "But you did."

Hayden's soulful brown eyes warmed back at me. "Goldie, I'd do anything for you."

"Anything?"

He sighed. "Yes. Anything."

"Would you catch a kangaroo for me?"

He smiled. "Yes."

"Would you catch a shooting star for me?"

He nodded. "Yes."

"How about the moon, Hayden?" I finished the rest of my drink and placed the glass besides his on table above us. "Would you catch the moon for me?"

Suddenly and without warning he swept me up into his arms and embraced me. "Goldie, now you're speaking my language. I've been after the man in the moon for a long time."

I could barely breathe. I nodded against him.

"You see, I think he's made of cheese."

I smiled.

"And I like cheese. And I like you," he said with his face inches from mine. "So I'd gladly catch a kangaroo for you and capture a thousand stars so you could have a thousand wishes. But maybe," he said as he leaned in for a kiss, "we could capture the man in the moon together?"

His mouth met mine in a deep, wonderful, passionate kiss.

"I'd like that," I said with my mouth next to his. "Because then really I would have everything."

"Goldie, I will give you everything you've ever wanted, and there'll probably be times I'll give you things you don't want, like an accidental fat lip and bruised wrists."

I shook my head. "Bring on the bruised wrists. And I'll install a doorbell."

He leaned his head against mine. "So we're good?"

I grinned with a laugh. "Hayden, we're better than good. We're amazing."

"I think so," he said with a confidence that made his chest expand before me. "Cinder Ella may have her prince, but Goldie Locks found her Bear."

"Yes, I did." I kissed him, and it felt like our souls connected.

"You're the one," he said softly in my ear. "It's always been you."

I leaned into him, and his tongue glided across my earlobe and lingered to nibble. His passion ignited a fire inside me that no man had ever kindled. I wanted more. My thighs trembled in anticipation. *Yes.*

I arched toward him and inhaled his scent of spice, timber, and evergreen. I wanted to rip off the rest of his clothes and climb his masculine body, mounting every inch that now flexed before me as he held me in his arms and gently, passionately played upon my neck. *Faster, harder, more.* But he took his time, sparking a flame that continued to grow with every touch, sending a shock wave reaction throughout my body with every touch.

Suddenly he stopped.

"I came here to report on a bar fight, so I still don't have a condom." His hand came up to wipe his face when I stopped it mid-stream.

"I do." I reached toward the trash can where my purse slung from the side and fished it off with my finger.

Hayden smiled. "Then what are you waiting for, woman? Take off your clothes."

I giggled, slid off my jacket and unbuttoned my coral blouse and tossed them both to the floor. My hair fell out of its pony tail and cascaded down my bare back.

"You're beautiful."

I stopped undressing beneath the oak table, and time stood still. I stared at Hayden, and Hayden stared at me. For a moment neither of us did anything but gaze into each other's eyes.

"So did you ever imagine that we'd end up here when we first met?" I said.

"Getting naked with you under a table in a tavern?" He shook his head. "No, I definitely didn't see that one coming."

I rolled his eyes. "Not that. You know what I mean. *Us.*"

Hayden gently reached for my hands. "Goldie, the first time I heard your voice, my mind went *here.* I wondered what it would be like to be with you like this." He paused. "Maybe not in a tavern, under a table." He smiled. "But when I heard your voice, I imagined this moment. And then I had to know who had claimed me simply by speaking into my earpiece."

Never before had my heart opened so widely and felt so full at the same time. It overflowed with an abundance that I knew would never run dry.

"I like you, too."

"Oh, I passed the 'Like Street' a long time ago," he said.

It wasn't possible for me to be happier. I leaned over kissed him gently and unzipped my jeans. Hayden pulled on the pant legs until they were off me. He threw them behind us.

"Nice. I've always wanted candle wax stains on my jeans," I said.

He reached for the center of my lilac bra where it clasped. "It'll match your belt burns."

I giggled. I wanted to stand before him in my lacy bra and black panties, but since standing wasn't an option I knelt before him. My nipples were taut, and my breasts were ripe for the taking. And my God, how I wanted him to take them.

He unclasped my bra, and my full breasts partially bounded out of their constraints. Lace lingered just along the edge of my nipple. I looked at my half-exposed breast and back up at him and smiled. He rolled the straps off each shoulder until the bra fell to the ground behind me.

His calloused hands slowly moved down the sides of my body grazing my breasts and peaked nipples. His hands cupped their shaped, while his thumb traced my areola and gently rubbed my nipple. It was an intoxicating combination and a hypotonic hit to the senses. I tilted my head back lost in the moment, but just as soon as I was in euphoric bliss he moved further down my body. He seemed to be physically memorizing the outline of my body, the contours of my curves, the low dip that led to the promise of fulfillment we hadn't been able to enjoy the other night. I wanted him to stake it, claim it, and own it.

My clit was peaked, ready to be touched, sucked, or whatever he wanted to do. I had to have him inside me, and the longer he made me wait the more my hunger for him grew.

Hayden took off his boots quickly.

"Impressive," I said.

"Some ER nurse taught me the value of prompt clothes removal," he said and then drew me into him. I wrapped my legs around his waist, waiting for the green light, waiting for him to pull back his belt buckle, unzip his jeans, and let the beast that I felt pressed hard against me come out of hibernation.

My body throbbed, and I ached with a pounding pulse that couldn't be ignored. I pressed into his jeans with hot, wet radiated heat that needed release. I glided my tongue across his bare chest and flicked each nipple until they stood at attention along with his cock. I reached down and dipped my hand into his jeans, grabbed his cock, and gave it a good, tight tug. I reached for his belt and zipper, and within seconds his cock sprang before me with a rich, thick, full head and ridged edges. I oozed knowing he would fulfill and satisfy me and my every desire, and right now my desire was to lick the drop of cum on the tip of his cock.

I shimmed down him and took a long, meaningful lick. He tasted bittersweet. I placed him in my mouth and started to live out every fantasy I had that began and ended with being with a man that not only loved me, but also loved satisfying me. Add to it one that had a huge, pleasing cock, and Hayden was a fantasy come true.

I jerked his cock with my hand and coated it with my mouth until it dripped with saliva before I reached into my purse, ripped open the condom and rolled it down his cock. Hayden looked at me.

"You were in charge of dessert last time," I said. "I figure it's my turn to pay it forward."

He grinned.

He started to finger me, but I lay down on the hardwood floor and directed him inside me. I gasped, and he groaned.

175

"Deeper," I said as I surrendered and he took over.

I clamped down on him and wouldn't let go while he moved deeper inside me. With each thrust I rubbed my clit in perfect rhythm with him. The combination paired with having sex under the table in the tavern spiked my arousal to levels I had never imagined. I gushed and his cock exploded, and together we erupted into multiple orgasms.

"Well, that was fast, furious, and probably over with too quickly for both of us," he said in my ear.

"Yes, but neither of us got burned by candle wax in the process," I said.

"True."

"Nor did I end up with a swollen lip, wrist burns, or any damage to my home," I said with my mouth pressed against his cheek. "So really it's a win-win."

Hayden leaned up, looked into my eyes and smiled. "You're right," he said and moved a piece of hair off my face. "By finishing that nasty drink, our luck has turned."

I smiled.

"And, Goldie," he said with a kiss, "it's only going to get better."

It felt like I was floating on air as I cuddled beside my favorite Bear of them all and fell asleep with dreams of happily ever after.

The End

www.pumpkinspicecom.wordpress.com

Evernight Publishing ®

www.evernightpublishing.com

Made in the USA
Charleston, SC
24 December 2016